Brownlow grabs my arm and starts pulling me down the corridor. 'Thank God you've come. You came by road, I suppose?'

'Well – yes.'

'You should have come by train. Another five minutes and they would have ripped the place apart.'

I can imagine the sce

nothing to drink it out o

'What is?'

'The glasses,' I say.

'Glasses?' Mr Brown

'You don't want glasses.

may go down all right

Nothing sophisticated u

you can forget about the glasses.'

Before I can ask him what he is talking about, Mr Brownlow stops outside a door. Through it I can hear what sounds like a female choir singing 'Why are we waiting?' Something tells me there is more to the Barnly Working Men's Club than meets the eye . . .

I take a deep breath. 'Listen Mr Brownjob,' I say. 'I think there's been a –'

The sound of 'Why are we waiting?' is joined by the uneven stamping of feet. Brownlow tightens his grip on the door knob. 'We can't wait any longer,' he says. 'You'll have to go on as you are. The panic button is on the right of the bongos . . .'

Also by Timothy Lea for
Futura Publications Ltd

CONFESSIONS FROM THE POP SCENE
CONFESSIONS FROM A HEALTH FARM
CONFESSIONS FROM THE SHOP FLOOR

Timothy Lea

Confessions of a Long Distance Lorry Driver

Futura Publications Limited

A Futura Book

First published in Great Britain in 1975
by Futura Publications Limited

ISBN 0 860 71804
Printed in Great Britain by
Hazell Watson & Viney Ltd
Aylesbury, Bucks

In respectful homage to the one and only Roger Carpenter and his fortunate bride.

Futura Publications Limited
49 Poland Street
London W1A 2LG

CONTENTS

Chapter Seven

In which Timmy and Sid are asked to remove nearly everything by an animated lady who wants her furniture taken to Peterborough.

Chapter Eight

In which Timmy and Sid find that they have been duped and are forced to take evasive action from a betrayed husband.

Chapter Nine

In which Timmy calls on a northern club and finds himself pressed into service by an all-female audience when the male strip-tease artist fails to put in an appearance.

Chapter Ten

In which snow falls and Timmy comes across an old friend.

CHAPTER ONE

In which Timmy escapes from a double bed floating in the Thames and is received aboard a Russian ship by Olga, the vessel's appropriately named Comfort Officer.

Two hundred yards downstream the bed sinks.

Typical, isn't it? I should have known the moment Sid asked me how I'd like to be the first man to sail round the world on a bed. Mind you, I would have thought that it might have stayed afloat for a bit longer – like to The Isle of Dogs or even Woolwich Ferry. Still, you can't afford that kind of naive optimism when you are dealing with my brother-in-law, Sidney Noggett. It is like buying a hot water bottle before you go for a paddle in the alligator pool.

The events leading up to Sid casting me adrift on a double bed – I was lucky it was a double, he isn't usually that generous – are well known to readers of *Confessions from the Shop Floor*, more an education than a book and still available from Futura Publications, or direct from me including seven pounds eighty-five pence for postage and packing. Suffice to say that Sid planned to use my trip round the world to publicise the firm of bedmakers he has bought his way into, The Universal International Bedding Company – now known as Slumbernog.

At the moment, it looks as if another great Noggett idea is about to make contact with the bed of the Thames. Not that the bed sinks fast, I will say that for it. In fact it takes me a few minutes to realise that the water is rising up the inside of my trouser leg. I thought it was the wash from a passing tug. To say that cold panic invades my system is no exaggeration. I can feel percy trying to find a foothold on my belly button as the icy water gets closer and closer. Thank goodness Sid left me with a life jacket. He is not all bad. There is a piece of string hanging down the front of it and some writing. What does it say? 'REJECT'. I wonder if that has anything to do with inflating it? Only one way to find out. I wrench the piece of string. There is a loud ripping noise and one side of the jacket comes away at the shoulder. Oh well, back to the drawing board. Maybe the pillows will keep me afloat – or maybe they would have done. The last one is floating off into the night.

Blimey! I am really getting worried now. You don't know how fast the current in the Thames can move until you try floating down it on a double bed. Sid must have chosen an ebb tide specially. Conniving bastard! I wish I had my hands on him now. His own brother-in-law. How could he do it?

I am on the point of losing contact with the bed when I look up and see a row of lights looming up in front of me. For a moment I think that I must have drifted in to shore. Then I can make out a mast and rigging against the night sky. It must be a boat.

'Help!' I shout, 'Man Overboard! Help!'

There is no faulting what I am shouting. It is all good solid stuff that I have seen used to very good effect on any number of telly screens. If my name was Robert Redford the water around me would look like an explosion in a washer factory as the lifebelts plopped over the side. But my name is Timothy Lea and that makes a lot of difference. All I hear is the echo of my own voice, the lonely hoot of a foghorn and a sound like someone playing the banjo. At least the boat in front of me does not appear to be moving. I had always reckoned on dying in bed, but not by being cut in half by a bleeding great liner!

I have hardly had time to open my cakehole again when – zomp! The bed bashes into the side of the boat and goes down faster than Britain's gold reserves. So much for the pride of the Noggett fleet. I fling out my arms and find myself clutching the thick links of a gunge-encrusted chain. For a few seconds the current plucks at my body and then I manage to haul myself up and find a foothold on the chain. Exciting, isn't it? I bet you are all on the edge of your seats. No? Well, do you mind edging forward a bit as I get discouraged very easily? Ta. Anyway, there I am, shivering with cold and terror and trying not to think why the anchor chain I am clinging to smells the way it does. All those rats running up and down it can't help a lot. I suck in a few deep breaths, square my enormous shoulders, and start struggling up to where the chain disappears through a hole in the side of the ship.

Above me, I can begin to make out the name of the boat. It looks like *Len Grade*. It must be named after one of the famous Grade family. Funny, I have heard of Lew and Leslie but not Len. As I get nearer I see that there is a lot of other writing, like the symbols they use in cartoons when someone is swearing, and that it is *Leningrad* not *Len Grade*. The boat must come from Russia which accounts for the balalaika music smiting my earholes. I thought it was a bit haunting for a banjo.

This news cools down my blood another couple of degrees. I know that the Ruskies do not take kindly to unannounced visitors snooping round their goodies and I hope that there are going to be no misunderstandings about the reason for my appearance on board. Better perhaps, if nobody knows about it. With this thought in mind, I slide my hand up the side of the boat and close my fingers round the lowermost of the rails. A few more contortions that Charles Atlas would envy – well, he must be about seventy now – and I pull myself up so that I can look on to the deck. There seems to be no one about so I swing my leg over the side and—

'Haltski! Stay exactly where you are!'

I wish the bloke with the gun had not said that because the ship's rail is threatening to carry the cleft in my arse round to the front of my body. 'I'm not a spy,' I say. 'My bed sank.'

'Your what?!'

'My boat sank,' I say. I mean, there is no point in making the confusion worse, is there? I flirt with a few items of verbal jollity that involve Vulgar Bedmen and Volgar Boatmen and decide against them. The gentlemen with the submachine-gun pointed at the centre of my nut cluster could well fail to be amused. Their ways are not our ways.

'You looking for asylum?'

What a funny thing to ask a bloke! I suppose I do look a bit odd but there is no reason to start jumping to conclusions. The geezer reads the expression of surprise on my face. 'I mean political asylum.'

'Oh, The House of Lords,' I say. 'You should have said. That's further up the river.'

'What is it Boris?' Another bloke rolls up wearing long boots and a fur hat. I wonder whether to tell him that his shirt has come out of his trousers but decide against it.

'I think it is another refugee from the fascist hyenas, Excellency.'

'Indeed.' The newcomer leans towards me and I suddenly tumble to the fact that it is a bird. I thought the voice was a bit funny. On closer inspection she reminds me of Vanessa Redgrave. You know, everything there, but stretched a bit. 'So, you want to go to Urals?'

'I wouldn't mind,' I say. You know how it is when you're

cold and you've had a few beers. It goes right through you.

'Come, follow me. I wish to examine your credentials.' I have heard how the Commies are great ones for spying on you but this is too much. Nobody follows me into the karsi. I am about to say something but the bird turns on her heel and the bloke gives me a playful nudge with his submachine-gun that clearly means 'get a move on'. In the circumstances I see no alternative but to do as I am nudged. I never reckoned myself with perforations.

Down some steps we go and along a narrow, dimly lit corridor that smells like a baby camel's chewing rag. The cold is now really getting through to me and I am shivering like your mum's automatic washing machine going into spin dry.

'You want to join the party?'

In my present condition, I have never felt less like a knees-up but I decide that it would be a bad idea to refuse the lady's invitation. 'Yeah, lovely,' I say. 'I wouldn't mind getting out of these things though.'

'Of course. Boris, get the comrade a people's suit.'

I am not sorry to see Boris taking his machine-gun for a walk and for a moment I consider making a bolt for it. Then it occurs to me that it probably has a bolt anyway. Plus a trigger and all the other bits. I will have to find another way of working myself into the Commie's favour.

'Do you know Nitya Pullova?' I say. 'She comes from Omsk.'

Comrade Pullova is the big knockered bird who has come to Slumbernog on an exchange visit and revolutionised production. So much so that the firm is actually making money and the horrible Rightberk brothers who share responsibility for spending all the profits with Sid have pushed off on a cruise. I throw that in just in case you like a bit of plot.

'Omsk?' says my companion, opening a cabin door with a wry smile – she uses her hand as well, of course. 'That is two thousand miles from Leningrad. London is nearer to Leningrad than Omsk.'

'Blimey,' I say. 'So it's right over the other side of the country?'

The bird smiles again. 'No, the beautiful city of Omsk is not even one third of the way across the Union of Soviet Socialist Republics.'

Amazing, isn't it? Nearly drowned and a free geography lesson into the bargain. Nobody can say that I don't lead a rich and varied life.

'Not surprising you don't know her then,' I say exhibiting once more the easy mastery of casual banter that has cemented my reputation as the Michael Parkinson of the West Clapham light ale and a packet of salt and vinegar crisps set.

There is a bit more light – of the electrical variety – in the sparsely furnished cabin and it gives me the opportunity to have a shufti at the bird. She looks a lot better when she has taken off her fur hat and allowed her blonde barnet to tumble round her shoulders. She has large grey eyes and a wide mouth that turns up temptingly at the corners. I would imagine that she is OK in the bristols department but it is a bit difficult to tell because of the blouse she is wearing. It has less shape than one of Mum's steak and kidney puddings. She is looking at my clobber with interest.

'You, serf,' she says.

'Not here,' I say. 'You need waves. You might be able to water ski but it wouldn't be much fun if you fell in. I mean, look at me.'

'I am looking at you.' She points to the front of my ripped life jacket. ' "REJECT". That is how your capitalist society designates you.'

It has been occurring to me that the word 'reject' might well refer to something else – like what the manufacturer thinks ought to be done with a garment that quite clearly fails to come up to scratch. I wonder where Sid got it from? Probably off the back of a lorry. So much of what Sid lays his hands on falls off the back of lorries that the items usually carry tyre marks.

'Take offski those sad rags.' The lady is swift to note the hesitation on my part, prompted by hundreds of years of genteel breeding and the certain knowledge that my brush with cold hearted Father Thames has resulted in my hampton taking on the proportions of a dwarf brussel sprout – Hampton Wick as you might say. 'Do not worry about exposing yourself to me. I have seen more naked men than you have had.'

I wait expectantly for her to say 'hot dinners' but she doesn't.

'What exactly do you do on board?' I ask, peeling off the remains of Sid's jacket. A card falls out of one of the pockets which says 'Everything slashed!' I don't think it referred only to the prices.

'I am Comfort Officer. I ensure that revolutionary fervour is maintained at high level and that crew have spotski of in and outski on Saturday night. Here, I do it.' So saying she briskly begins to peel off my sodden clobber like she is removing washing from a line.

'Blimey,' I say. 'All on Saturday night?! Have you considered staggering?'

'I don't have to consider,' she says with feeling. 'I stagger!'

The feeling I am referring to is what might be termed a

brisk massage and richochets through the lower half of my body like honey bullets. The lady is obviously well-equipped with the physical wherewithal to withstand the passionate demands of the crew and it occurs to me that the work is probably no hardship to her. 'I do not know what has happened to Boris,' she says, whipping down my Y-fronts. 'Maybe you like to lie down. You like bunk up?'

'I beg your pardon!' I say. I mean, I am not used to girls being so forward. This isn't a Young Conservatives' dance or anything like that.

'You like bunk up or bunk down?' The Russian lady is now pointing to the two bunks in the cabin and her meaning becomes clear to me.

'The bottom one's fine,' I say, grabbing a blanket and adjusting my shapely limbs in a horizontal position.

Before there is time for any more sparkling interchanges the cabin door opens and Boris reappears with a bundle of clothing. 'Is that all, Excellency?'

There is a note of pleading in his voice that goes unheeded.

'Yes Boris. Go and read the library book.'

'But Olga, Excellency. I know the life of Karl Marx backwards. I have other needs.'

'They will be attended to, Boris. Now leave us.'

The door closes on the resentful Boris and Olga looks at her watch. 'So,' she says. 'It is now Saturday.'

'Yes,' I say, trying to keep the conversation bubbling along. 'I like the weekends.'

'I prefer the strong ends,' says Olga. 'They make my job so much easier.'

'I don't think you quite understood what I mean,' I say. 'I was referring to – oh well, it doesn't really matter.'

Olga has suddenly pulled her shift over her head to reveal that my hopes for her knockers were well founded.

Naked as nature intended they lunge forward like a couple of gently curved hunting horns. The angle of dangle is tempting and my own horn starts thinking about doing a bit of hunting.

Olga picks up a bottle and a couple of glasses and sits on the edge of my bunk. 'Now you are one of us you are entitled to take pleasure from my body like any other crude member' – I think she means crew member but I don't say anything. You can't go on picking people up all the time, can you? It is very clever of her to be able to speak English as well as she does.

'That's very nice of you,' I say. 'But—' I am about to say that there has been some kind of mistake and that I am not running away from anything and that I don't want to join the crew when I remember the expression on Boris's face as he went out of the door. It was not projecting a lot of human warmth and affection in my direction and could easily suggest an unbalanced personality with a quick trigger finger.

'Yes?' says Olga.

'Nothing,' I say. 'I was just thinking.'

Olga pours some colourless liquid into a glass and hands it to me. 'Maybe you think too much. From now on, we do thinking for you.'

'What is this?' I say.

'Just straightforward party philosophy.'

'I meant the drink,' I say.

'Wodka.'

'You mean vodka?'

'I mean wodka.'

I take a sip and she is obviously right. It is wodka. Potent too. I have already consumed a bellyful of booze earlier in the evening and this stuff races through me like a flaming brand in a paraffin factory.

'You like?' Her knockers are now brushing against my bare chest and the sensation serves to short circuit the current already pumping through me from the wodka – the stuff must be pure anti-freeze.

'I like.' I put my glass on the floor and allow my mouth the freedom of Olga's cakehole. With a gentleness for which I am grateful she returns the pressure and presses her warm bristols against my chest. I don't know if you have ever seen a carp sucking at a piece of bread on the surface of a pond but that is rather her kissing style. A lot of gentle chewing and the occasional gnaw of the lower lip.

We go on like this for a while and she wriggles on to the bunk so that she is stretched out on top of me. It is very good for the warming up and after a few minutes of our nibble fest the last icicles have thawed and percy is rising like an early crocus from the melting snow. In fact, when I say crocus I do man's best friend a disservice. He is coming up more like a scarlet cucumber.

A woman like Olga is clearly no stranger to the effect that she has on men and it is not many seconds after percy has thrust himself between us that she lets out an exclamation that sounds like the name of a new Japanese motor bike and begins to sew kisses on my chest like they are mustard seed. I watch her tawny barnet taxiing down to the root of many of my problems and it occurs to me that something very pleasant is about to happen to Timothy. 'Oh!' That is me responding to Olga's snake tongue trying to undo my belly button. 'Oooh!' Olga's right hand has now coasted up the inside of my thigh and is gently squeezing my niagras like they are the bellows which inflate my already straining Mad Mick. 'OOOH!!' Olga has now done something very volga that you seldom see unless you watch the chocolate bar commercials on the telly. How shameless and enjoyable it all is. As the minutes pass and Olga's bobbing nut becomes increasingly in danger of bashing itself against the upper bunk, I decide that is is about time that I did something to repay the hospitality that I am being offered. It is no good lying back and expecting to have everything done for you. Do as you would consider yourself very fortunate to be done by is one of my mottoes.

Not without some regret, I draw Olga up my body and reapply myself to her lips whilst attempting to remove the garments which lumber the lower half of her body. They obviously do things up differently in Russia because I am not getting anywhere until my friend jumps from the bed, tears open her breeches, tugs off her boots and leaps on top of me again. Such eagerness is touching, as are most parts of her body. With some difficulty, I press her back against the wall and adjust my cakehole to the nearest available knocker. This treatment is well received by the lady and it is with little difficulty that I persuade her to enjoy every knocker's favourite meal – guzzle and tweak. I dish out a second helping to each Manchester and then head south like a migrating swallow – or dipper, more like. It is funny how birds – I mean the human kind – work themselves up when a muff job is in the air, isn't it? Backs arch, heads twist from side to side before you have even licked your lips. Olga is no exception. By the time I have found a way of propping my legs against the far wall of the cabin and swept the hair out of my eyes, you could run a model railway under her back. Mind you, it would be a terrible waste if you did. You can play with your model railway any day of the week. A girlchick like Olga comes along only when Sid casts you adrift on a double bed. And that, thank God, is not very often. As Olga quivers I set my tongue to work like it is a bow playing a musical instrument. I can't say I recognise the tune that comes out but it is certainly a very cheerful sound. Ideally, I reckon that a muff job is a horse's duvet (hors d'oeuvres? Ed.) It should wet the appetite for what is to come and get the old gastric juices flowing. I don't think it ought to become a meal in itself.

Anyway, in this case, everything works out just about right. Olga suddenly arches her back and catches her nut a terrible crack on the upstairs bunk and I realise that she is trying to tell me something. Hardly before she has sunk back against the pillow, I have stopped staring at the small hammer and sickle she has tattooed above her minge fringe and have hauled myself up her body until percy is now poised for his journey into the interior. I often wonder how he must feel at moments like this. So many responsibilities to discharge, his two porters struggling along behind him – one slightly in front of the other – and the secret cave looming in front, thick foliage almost concealing its narrow opening. It is nearly as exciting as *King Solomon's Mines*, isn't it?

'Comeski, my little comrade.'

I am not so happy about the little but I assume that it is merely a term of affection. Better not to dwell on it. Wishing that my knees had ridges, I murmur a silent farewell to my fanny ferret and jerk forward the part of my anatomy that carries the six inch gun. Olga's response is whole-hearted and suggests that she has played this game before. Faster than a camera shutter, her mits clamp round my back ballast and she presses me to her like she wants to take a moulding of my body. At the same moment her legs curve round outside mine and hook over my ankles. It looks like the perfect fall and I can almost hear the referee counting and Kent Walton doing his nut. The Commie custard is now rotating my bum like she is trying to unscrew it. Maybe this has something to do with the counter revolution she was talking about earlier.

This is all very well but, once again, I feel that I should stamp my own personality on the proceedings. After all, I am representing Britain and regular readers will know that I always pull out all the stops when national prestige is at stake. If we all did our bit – or, in fact, anybody's bit – then maybe this dear old country of ours would not be in the mess it is now. At the very least, life would be a lot more fun.

Rising up so that my bonce loosens three of the slats in the upstairs bunk, I drive viciously and feel the satisfying 'thwack!' of my baggage train against Olga's back bumpers. Bracing my toes against the end of the bunk, I deal out a few telling thrusts and hear the satisfying sound of Olga searching for breath. Her hands run lightly up my back as if she is playing a harp and I accompany her on the trombone – in, out; in, out, in – you can't beat a musical evening.

Half an hour later, we are still at it, but on the floor this time. The bunks have collapsed. In my present condition, I can't imagine what it felt like to be cold. Rivulets of condensation are running down the steamed up porthole and the wodka bottle is warm to the touch – when you can touch it. Olga is kneeling on all fours and taking hefty swigs interspersed by shouts of 'Giddyupski!'. I am in a position slightly to the rear of the lady and we are playing a game she describes as 'Sleigh rides'. She is between the shafts as she terms it and I must say that it is something that I envy her. I have not been 'between the shafts' since we started this bout of intensive, not to mention knackering, exercise and the strain is beginning to tell.

'Once more up and down the Caucasus!' says my hostess gaily. Frankly, I would be pushed to get up and down the crocuses. It is all I can do to prolong my attachment to the lady as she bumps and grinds round the floor.

Fortunately, some strange whim makes her suddenly flip over on to her back and seize me to her greedily. 'Ride me, little moujik,' she cries. 'Ride me!'

Sensing that the moment has come, I decide to follow suit. Summoning up my last resources of energy I whip the old groin greyhound in and out until he makes Mick the Miller look like your grandma's tabby cat. Olga lets out a wild shriek and grabs my barnet like she has Red Indian blood in her. I chuck in a few croaks and in a classic fusion of Eastern and Western ideologies, mutual orgasm is achieved. Olga lets out what I can only describe as a contented sigh and her head zonks back against the carpet. She makes a few purring noises and then starts snoring. A glance at the quarter of inch of liquid left in the bottom of the wodka bottle suggests that is is not only the compulsive fire of my love-making that is responsible for her condition.

This may well be the moment to say goodbye. Olga was not amused when I told her that I thought the Red Square was a geezer called Brezhnev and it is clear that there is another side to her nature that I have not been fully exposed to. Life with Olga would not purely be a question of getting tossed off in Rostov.

Whilst my fair companion snuggles closer to her wodka bottle I slip into the threads provided by Boris. They may go down a bomb in the Stalingradski Prospect but I don't reckon that they are going to pull a lot of birds down the baths hall. Still, that is not my number one problem at the moment. Blowing what I hope is a farewell kiss to the toast of the Neva, I ease open the cabin door and stick my hooter out into the corridor. Not a sausage. Less sign of a human being than there is of a knot in a Scotsman's used french letter – at least, that is, until I start walking down the corridor. Then Boris's boots appear down the steps, closely followed by the rest of his body. He eyes me suspiciously and the nozzle of his submachine-gun starts giving percy palpitations.

'There you are!' I say in a flash of creative desperation. 'I've been looking for you everywhere. Olga wants you.'

The way I say 'wants you' must make it clear to him that she is not seeking someone to unblock a stuffed up plughole.

'Me?' Boris's chest swells visibly. I don't know about the rest of him, I don't look.

'She's waiting for you in the cabin.' I just have time to flatten myself against the wall before Boris charges past. Cupid Lea they call me.

I don't hang about but canter up the steps and stick my bonce above deck level. Still no sign of anyone. I can hear the strain – and it is a strain, make no mistake about it – of an old Russian folk tune coming from the front of the boat. The crew must be having a musical evening. Good luck to them. Over to the rail I go and look over the side. As if to signal my good fortune the moon comes out and there, shimmering beside my reflection, is the outline of a dinghy. I take another quick glance about me and slip over the side. Fortunately, I manage to cling on to a rope before I do myself a serious injury. A few moments dangerous dangling and my feet scrabble against the side of the dinghy and manoeuvre it beneath me – it's not getting too exciting for you is it? Good. I wouldn't like to think that I was doing Alistair MacLean out of a living. Anyway, there I am, poised over the dinghy. The strength in my arms gives out and I tumble into the bottom of the boat. For a moment, it rocks alarmingly and then settles down to tap angrily against the side of the larger vessel. Quickly,

I undo the piece of rope at the sharp end, and push off with one of the oars.

Free! What an evening for my treasure trove of memories. The dinghy drifts down the side of the boat and I prepare to row to the shore. Most of the portholes show round circles of light but one has a pair of bum knockers jammed up against it. I imagine that Boris must be enjoying his Saturday constitutional.

CHAPTER TWO

In which Timmy and brother-in-law, Sid, set out to purchase a haulage business and share a few tremulous moments with Suzanne and Babs – amongst others.

In the end it is eight o'clock in the morning by the time I get round to Sid's place in trendy Vauxhall. The blooming current carried me all the way round to Plumstead Marshes before I was able to get ashore.

I am not in a good mood and it is with no little force that I bang on the heavy brass doorknocker. Frankly, I am surprised that nobody has nicked it. When they moved in, Rosie said that the area was coming up but a glance around suggests that most of it is coming down – either falling or being pulled. Looks like Sid got lumbered again. It is no good being the only house in the street with a lilac front door if it has 'Poufdah!' written on it with an aerosol paint spray. The door opens and there is Rosie wearing a black robe with Chinese dragons all over it. She is carrying a glass of orange juice.

'You're not having another kid, are you?' I say, clocking the mitful of vitamin C.

'Of course I'm not! I'm having my breakfast. What are you doing round here?'

'I'm looking for Sid,' I say, pushing past the colour supplement life-style and entering the house. Rosie has changed a lot since she got into the boutiques and wine bars. You would never catch her drinking orange juice for breakfast in the old days. Then it was a cup of tea and a marmite sandwich.

'You might wipe your feet,' she says. 'And why are you wearing that ridiculous suit?'

I don't answer her because I have just clapped eyes on Sid. He is sitting at a scrubbed pine table and reading a glossy brochure entitled *Jetsetter Holidays in Brazil*.

A puzzled and unhappy expression settles over his face as he sees me. 'What are you doing here?' he says.

'I just walked from the Copacabana Beach,' I tell him. 'You can forget that for a start. "Drift across the Atlantic and taxi down the coast of South America to Rio de Janeiro." I should cocoa!'

'Are you coming, too?' says Rosie. 'Sid never tells me anything.'

'I was going on ahead,' I say. 'By sea. I don't suppose Sid told you that?'

'He said he had to meet someone,' says Rosie. 'What is all this?'

'Where's the bed?' says Sid. 'You haven't damaged it, have you? I sunk a lot of investment in that.'

'You sunk it to the bottom of the Thames,' I say. 'It didn't stay afloat more than a couple of hundred yards. It's a miracle that I'm alive!'

Sid claps his hands to his head. 'Gordon Bennett! I might have guessed you'd make a mess of everything. What is it about you?'

'What are you two talking about?' says Rosie.

'Sid wanted me to drift round the world on a floating bed,' I tell her. 'The trouble was that it didn't float.'

'You didn't have to drift,' says Sid. 'You could have rowed a bit. Your attitude's typical of so many young people today. You want everything on a plate. It's getting so a kid expects a Duke of Edinburgh Award for pulling out a sheet of bog paper.'

'Drifting round the world on a bed?' echoes Rosie. 'That's dangerous.'

'Oh belt up!' snaps Sid. 'If you want to say anything you can blame your perishing brother for putting the mockers on our holiday.'

'What do you mean?' says Rosie.

'I can't charge it to expenses if he hasn't gone, can I? Just think about it. We might have had to wait there for months until he showed up.'

A glance at Rosie shows me that she is torn by what I have heard described as conflicting emotions. 'We're not going?' she says. 'But I've got all the clothes.'

Sid shrugs. 'You'll have to send them back to Carmen Miranda's estate, won't you?'

Rosie turns to me. 'Are you sure you didn't act a bit hastily, Timmy?'

'I acted hastily, all right!' I say. 'If I hadn't, it would be my corpse standing here! You don't seem to understand the seriousness of what I'm telling you. I was nearly sent to my death.'

'And I'd set my heart on it, too,' says Rosie, sinking into a chair – for a moment, I think she is talking about me kicking the bucket.

'You know who to blame,' sulks Sid, wiping his cake-hole on the tablecloth and picking up his golf putter.

'It's not fair, those Rightberks gallivanting round the world while we can't go anywhere. I thought you'd bought control of the firm?' Rosie looks at Sid accusingly.

'Yeah, so did I, but it's more complicated than that.' Sid puts a glass on the floor and prepares to tap golf balls into it. I would have chosen one that was not half full of orange juice, myself, but I have noticed before that Sid is inclined to get flustered when Rosie starts having a go at him.

'Mind what you're doing, you great pillock!' It is sad

to hear Rosie talking like that. I can remember the time when she used to think that the sun went in every time Sid zipped up his fly.

'Belt up, slug nipples!' It is clear that feelings are running high and I am not sorry when there is a sharp rat-tat-tat on the front door.

'I'll get it,' I say.

The sound of battle is still ringing in my lugholes as I swing open the door and find myself staring at the back of the postman's head.

'Hello, darling,' he says, giving my left nipple a playful tweak. 'Look at those naughty doggies. I wouldn't mind having a bit of that, would you?'

'Why don't you ask one of them?' I say.

The bloke whips round and turns an interesting shade of scarlet. 'Oh yes-er. Recorded delivery,' he says, shoving a pencil stub and a piece of paper into my hand. 'Sign here.' He looks me up and down questioningly. 'Are you an au pair boy?'

The sooner I get out of this tunic the better. It does make me look like a blooming waiter. 'That's right,' I say. 'You're the commandant of the Boys' Brigade, aren't you?'

'Watch it!' The bloke is swift to take umbrage.

'You want to watch your hands, and all!" I take the letter and close the door firmly in his face. Honestly, I don't know what public servants are coming to these days. It makes me glad that I still have his pencil.

'What is it?' says Sid, as I go into the room. 'Another bleeding bill?'

'I don't think so,' I say. 'It's got a French stamp on it.'

'That doesn't mean anything,' says Sid. 'Now we're in the Common Market I'm probably paying French taxes. Give it here!' He wrenches it open and I watch his lips begin to move as he tries to get his mouth round the words.

I wonder who could be writing to Sid from France? 'Blimey!'

I don't know if you have ever seen a bloke's face turn ashen but that is what happens to Sid's mug. All the colour drains out of it.

'What's the matter, Sid?'

'They can't do it!'

He lets the letter flutter to the ground and I pick it up. The notepaper crackles like a new fiver and is headed 'Villa Splendide, Cap des Riches, Cote d'Azur'. I look down the bottom of the letter and it is signed 'Plantagenet Rightberk'. It is not an easy letter to understand, but basically the meaning is clear: Sid is out on his ear.

'Just when I was coming to grips with my slice,' he whines. 'It's tragic.'

'Don't take it too hard, Sid,' I say. 'They are offering you a golden handshake.'

'Golden handshake?' Sid's features crumple up like a sheet of baking foil. 'It's more like a clip round the lug-hole with a piece of lead piping! Taking inflation into account, it's less than what I put into the business.'

'You haven't made a mess of it again, have you?' says Rosie speaking my mind for me. 'Really! You're like a big soft kid. You want to get yourself an accountant and a solicitor if you're going into business.'

'You can't trust them,' snaps Sid. 'They'll bleed you dry and take you to the cleaners.'

'At least, that way, they won't get blood over the machines,' I say.

Sid is not amused. 'Shut up!' he says. 'There's nothing funny about this. Seeing a noble lion dragged down by a pack of jackals is a tragic spectacle.'

There is much more in this vein followed by threats of legal action, letters to MPs and a bunch of fives up the hooter, but by half past three Sid is off to bullock (bullock's horn: pawn) his golf clubs and sign on at the labour. I feel sorry for him, but not so sorry that I offer to break open my piggy bank with my Xmas club. Years of experience suggests to me that it will not be long before Sid comes up with another imaginative and foolproof way of losing money.

Two evenings later, I am proved correct. We are sitting in the saloon bar of the Highwayman – all the toffs go in the public bar, these days, because they reckon it's where the locals hang out – and I am allowing the maestro of moan to treat me to a pint and a torrent of ear-bending rabbit about how badly he has been put upon.

'Sometimes, I feel like chucking it all in,' he says. I can't help wondering what 'it' he is talking about but I don't say anything. 'It's no good belonging to a large organisation in this country. If you're a boss then you can't get anyone to work for you and if you're a worker then the bosses are trying to exploit you all the time. People don't have any confidence in each other any more.'

'That's my pint you're drinking,' I say.

Sid puts the glass down and wipes his mouth with the back of his hand. 'Are you sure?' he says, suspiciously.

'Positive,' I say. 'You know that bloke who went to the karsi?'

'I don't know him,' says Sid.

'I thought you must do,' I said. 'You'd drunk half his pint before he even stood up.'

Sid picks up his empty glass, looks round nervously and starts edging down the bench. 'Big bloke, wasn't he?' he says. I nod. 'Just shows how overwrought I am. I don't know what I'm doing.'

'I'd better get you another pint to help calm your nerves, hadn't I?' I say.

Sid nods. 'Ta. I think a Mahatma Ghandi might slip down all right now you make me think of it.'

'Instead of?' I ask.

'No, as well as. I can't drink brandy by itself.'

'You poor bastard,' I say. 'You really suffer, don't you?'

Sid is never swift to detect when one is being sarcastical and he merely nods and starts prospecting for crunched up crisps in the bottom of a discarded packet. I get the drinks in and notice that the big fella has come back from the karsi – you would hope him to, wouldn't you? – and is looking at Sid and his empty glass with equal interest.

'Ta,' says Sid when I get back to the table. 'You know, I've been thinking.'

'I'm not certain it suits you,' I say.

'About what I was talking about earlier,' says Sid. 'I reckon the only thing to do is to be your own governor. That way, nobody can let you down or mess you about. You're responsible for everything that happens.' A faraway look comes into his eye. 'You remember what it was like when we were cleaning windows?'

'You mean, all those birds?'

Sid frowns. 'I wasn't referring to that. I was talking about how easy it was.'

'It was pretty easy with the birds,' I remind him.

'No forms, no taxes, no clocking on, knock off when you like.'

'And who you like,' I chip in.

'Money isn't everything. I've said that before.'

'You say it every time you're skint,' I remind him. 'There's two lots of people who never worry about mazuma: those who've got so much of it they don't know what to do with it and those who haven't got any.'

'Very philatelical,' says Sid. 'But, frankly, I'm not interested in what you pick up from those religious programmes before the Sunday film. It's job satisfaction I'm after.'

'Hear, hear!' The words do not issue from my shapely cakehole but from the big geezer whose beer Sid nicked. He is leaning towards us with an expression on his face that can only be described as rapt. 'I couldn't help overhearing what you were saying because I was listening very carefully,' he says apologetically. 'It's seldom that I find myself in such complete and utter agreement with anyone.'

'Ta, that's very nice of you,' says Sid. 'Would you care for a drop of something? I'm certain my friend here would be happy to—'

To my relief, the bloke holds up a hand. 'Thank you, but no. I hardly touch the stuff.' That is certainly true when you have Sid sitting next to you. The bloke smiles and shakes his head admiringly. 'Working for yourself, it's the only way. I ought to know.'

'You've got your own business, have you?' asks Sid.

The bloke's face clouds over. 'Not for much longer, I'm afraid.'

'It's not easy these days, is it?' says Sid, putting on his head mourner face.

'It's not that,' says the bloke. 'The business is going like a bomb. It's the wife.'

'Oh, I'm sorry,' says Sid. 'She's-er, um-er, has she?'

'Nothing like that,' says the bloke. 'She wants us all to go to Australia. Our eldest girl married an Australian. She kept writing all these letters and it got Mavis going. Now we're off. I've got to sell up.'

'Your wife's adamant, is she?' says Sid.

'No, C of E, but it doesn't matter out there as long as you're not black. She hasn't half made up her mind, though. Every morning she's in the back garden with her boomerang. She can throw it right round the house and make it come back again. You wouldn't credit it unless you'd clocked it coming in through the front gate. The vicar copped it right behind the earhole.'

'Fascinating,' says Sid. 'Tell me, what is the business?'

'Road haulage,' says the bloke. 'We've got a couple of lorries and we freelance round the country. Marvellous way of seeing a bit of scenery and getting paid for it. It's like a caravan holiday sometimes.'

I should be warned when I see mist rising from Sid's mince pies.

'It's just you, is it?' he says.

'Me and my boy. We're our own bosses, work when we like. I don't mind telling you, I'm going to miss it. Nice little business it was. Some lucky bloke's going to get a bargain.'

'About time we moved on, isn't it Sid?' I say.

'Belt up!' Sid doesn't even look at me. 'You haven't sold up yet?'

'No, they only confirmed the travel arrangements yesterday. I haven't had much time to think about it. I suppose I'll have to put an advertisement in the paper.'

'Probably the best idea,' I say, starting to stand up. 'I hope you—'

'Sit down!' Sid yanks me down beside him and leans forward eagerly. 'Well, Mr—'

'Rogers,' says the bloke. 'William Rogers.'

'Well, Mr Rogers.' Sid takes a deep breath. 'I'm very interested in what you've just said. I think we might be able to come to some arrangement.'

'You know somebody who might be interested?' says Mr Rogers.

'*I'm* very interested,' says Sid with the finality of a

corpse pulling the coffin lid down on itself. 'Are you sure you won't have a drink?'

'Oh well, maybe just this once. I'll have a scotch, ta.'

'A large one?' says Sid.

'Well – ta.'

Needless to say, it is Timothy Sucker who is despatched to buy the 'I'm so frisky' while Sid and Rogers practically hold hands under the table. There is something about the Rogers bloke that I don't trust. For a start off, anyone who has listened closely to Sid for a few minutes and is still prepared to do business with him must be round the twist. There is also the way he handles the scotch. He throws it down his throat like he is trying to knock a spot off the bottom of his Cousin Kelly. It does not square up with the image of a bloke who hardly touches the stuff.

'Ta,' he says, slapping his glass down on the table. 'Well, that's all settled then. My girls will show you the merchandise.'

'Settled?' I say.

'Yes,' says Sid. 'You know me. I don't mess about. I've agreed a very reasonable price with Mr Rogers and his daughters are going to take us round the garage.'

'I wish I could do it myself,' says Mr R. 'But the wife's mother is coming round and I want to be at the bedside in case she says anything. You know what they're like. They read unpleasantness into anything. I didn't know she was in the garage when I was trying to back the car in.'

'I thought your daughter was in Australia?' I say.

'The eldest one,' says Mr Rogers. 'You don't miss a trick do you, sonny?' He gives me a look that is so old-fashioned that it is practically wearing woad.

'Don't take any notice of him,' says Sid, kicking me in the ankle. 'He's seen too many Perry Mason programmes. Now, let us know where we can link up with your girls and we'll start the ball rolling. I must say, I'm very excited about this.'

Another large scotch later, Mr Rogers has made a telephone call to alert his daughters and is informing us of the address to go to. 'It would be a big help if you could pay in cash,' he says. 'I don't want to get clobbered for a lot of tax just before I leave the country.'

'You'll have to give us a bit of a reduction,' says Sid.

Mr Rogers whistles through his teeth. 'You strike a vicious bargain, don't you? I can see you're no mug.'

Sid looks pleased with himself but I have my doubts as to whether Mr Rogers's assessment is either genuine or correct.

Half an hour later, my doubts are even greater. Sid and I are rattling the fencing that surrounds a bomb site in British North Battersea. It also surrounds what looks like a scrap metal dump but is apparently the home of 'Squaredeal Used Cars'.

'This can't be the place,' I say. 'Let's go home, Sid.'

'Belt up,' says Sid. 'The bloke said they shared the premises, didn't he? I wonder if that's them, over there?'

'You mean, those two clapped out old wrecks?' I say, staring at a couple of ancient lorries rusting away in one of the railway arches.

'That's not a nice way to talk about two charming young ladies.'

I spin round and see that Sid was referring to a couple of birds who are hurrying towards us. They look as if they are no strangers to the make-up counter of Boots and are clearly not of a shy and retiring disposition.

'Hello, boys,' says the one in the scarlet plastic mac. 'I'm Babs and this is Suzanne. Sorry we're late. Did Fred – I mean, Dad, give you the key?'

'No,' says Sid. 'I'm Sid and this is my assistant, Timmy.

Why are you looking at me like that?'

The bird called Suzanne is indeed staring into Sid's mug like it is a 'What the butler saw' machine. 'It must be the light,' she says. 'It's uncanny.'

'You saw *The Exorcist* too, did you?' I say. 'A lot of people have commented.'

'Paul Newman,' she breathes. 'What do you think Babs?'

'I think he's more like Steve McQueen, myself,' says the other bird. 'Either way, it's very distracting. How can you be expected to do business with a bloke whose irresistible magnetism reduces you to a shapeless jelly?'

'Not shapeless,' says Sid gallantly.

'He makes Dave Allen sound like Alf Ramsey,' simpers Suzanne.

'How are we going to get in?' I say, deciding that my stomach can't take much more.

'We'll have to climb over the top,' says Babs. 'Give us a leg up, Suzanne.'

Without another word, the bird proceeds to insert one of her feet in the mesh and reveal as much of herself as she can while straddling the swaying fence. She is wearing stockings with a black rose on the suspender straps and frilly red panties, I can tell you that without sending for my magnifying glass.

'Careful,' says Sid. 'You don't want to do yourself an injury.'

'It's you who wants to be careful,' says Suzanne. 'You've got more to lose than we have.' With these saucy words the bird in the shorty fur coat with the bald patches proceeds to follow her sister over the fence.

'Hold on, I'll give you a hand.'

'Oooh!!'

'Sorry,' says Sid. 'I didn't mean to do that.'

'That's all right,' says Suzanne. 'Your hand was a bit cold, that's all.'

'Sid!' I whisper. 'You're not taking these girls seriously, are you? They look as if they're on the game.'

'You mind your language!' Sid is bristling like a turkey's cock. 'Just because they reckon me, there's no need to let your naked envy show through.'

It is no good trying to reason with Sid when he is in one of his moods and I say nothing but follow him over the fence. It's a good job there aren't any bules about because they might entertain suspicions.

'Here we are,' says Babs. 'This was the best model they ever made, you know. After 1955 they started introducing plastic components.' She leans against one of the mudguards which falls to the ground in a shower of dust.'

'Every part replaceable. It's so much easier if you do have a little accident. With some of these modern ones you have to buy half a lorry if something goes wrong.'

'Just in case we do have a prang,' I say, 'Where's the nearest blacksmith's?'

Babs looks at me coldly. 'Daddykins said you were sarcastic.'

'Don't mind him,' says Sid. 'I make the decisions round here.'

'I should think you could make anything round here,' says Suzanne running her fingers up the sleeve of Sid's Gannex.

'Do you want to get the feeling of the controls?' says Babs. 'It's lovely and snug inside. Do you remember when Daddy used to give us a ride, Suzanne?'

'That's where they score over the modern ones,' says Suzanne. 'They don't sacrifice the comfort. After all, you're going to spend a lot of time in the cab, aren't you? You might as well be cosy.'

Sid is obviously going to be like warm putty in these birds' hands and it is with something approaching eagerness that he wrenches open one of the doors. Fortunately, I step to one side just in time and the hunk of crumbling metal crashes harmlessly at my feet.

'Do you want to see the controls?' Suzanne is addressing me as if she does not care very much one way or the other.

'It has some, does it?' I say. 'I thought maybe you pressed up and down on a couple of pedals.'

'Oh my, we are funny, aren't we? Proper little comedian.'

Sid has scrambled into the cab in a cloud of rust and Babs is following, showing everything she has got and a bit more she must have borrowed from someone else. It occurs to me that they may not be re-emerging in a hurry and that I might be wise to take advantage of what shelter is available. It is very parky on the bomb site.

'Come on, then,' I say. 'Let's have a look at it.' I open the door – very carefully – and pull myself up into the second of the two relics of the golden years of the British motor industry. 'You're very high off the ground, aren't you?' I say, as the bird climbs in beside me.

'What do you mean! ? I'm just over five foot.'

'Not you,' I say patiently. 'I was referring to the height of the cab from the ground.'

'Oh yes,' she says. 'It's nice, isn't it? Nice arrangement of dials and all that.'

'Do you know what they all do?' I ask.

'I know where the heater switch is.' She leans forward and turns a knob. The windscreen wipers start scratching backwards and forwards with a high-pitched squeaking noise.

'Interesting,' I say, 'I suppose the friction heats up the

windscreen and it slowly spreads through the whole lorry?'

'You are unkind,' she says. 'I'm not Graham Hill.'

'No, he's got a moustache, hasn't he?' I say. 'Look, I'm not expecting mechanical wizardry but you're supposed to be selling me this crate. I don't reckon you even know how to start it.'

For a moment, I think the bird is going to clock me. Then, she pulls open the glove compartment and shoves a key in my mit. 'You start it.'

'Where do I put this?' I say, indicating the key.

'I know where I'd like you to put it,' says the bird.

'I wouldn't want to run the risk of hurting you,' I say. 'Let's try this hole here. It looks a bit smaller.'

Before she can really get into her stride, mouth-wise, I insert the key in the ignition and turn it in a clockwise direction. To my surprise, there is a noise like my bronchitic Uncle Norman clearing his throat into a megaphone and the engine slowly roars into life.

'There you are, clever dick!' says Suzanne drawing her legs up underneath her. 'I bet that shook you.'

'I bet it shook you and all,' I say. I twiddle one of the other knobs and there is a smell of burning dust and old mouse droppings, combined with a current of warm air around turn-up level.

'There, you see! Everything works.'

I don't say anything but I have to confess that the old bus has a kind of bashed up charm about it. The seats are so shiny that they might have perspex over them and all the numerals on the dials are picked out in old-fashioned lettering. I can quite see myself chugging round the countryside in this. It is practically a collector's piece.

'Well, what do you think?'

The bird has turned to face me and is brushing a wisp of hair out of her eyes. Curled up on the seat she looks quite attractive. Small but well constructed. The fur coat has flopped open and I can see the soft swelling of one of her knockers slotted into the top of her dress.

'Not bad,' I say.

'It's warm, isn't it?'

She is right, it is warm. I look beyond her to the driving cab of the lorry Sid is in. The window is steamed up and I can just make out the imprint of two upside down boots. Sid always was a fast worker.

'Do you think you're going to like it, Down Under?' I ask her.

The bird gives me a playful nudge. 'You don't mind what you say, do you?'

'That's what they call it, isn't it?' I say.

'I dunno,' says Suzanne. 'They call it so many things, don't they?'

'I suppose they do,' I say. To tell the truth I can't think of anything else other than 'down under' or 'Aussie'. There is some word like 'antipathies' but I don't reckon she could be referring to that. She doesn't immediately strike you as a likely candidate for 'Mastermind'. 'How about your sister, is she looking forward to it?' Suzanne glances towards the next door lorry. 'Not any more,' she says. I follow her eyes and wonder if we are talking about the same thing. The window is now open and a female leg is hanging out of it. It waves grotesquely and then is joined by Sid's. I must remind him to get that hole in his sole mended.

'It is warm in here, isn't it?' I say.

Suzanne takes a deep breath and leans towards me sticking out her lower lip. 'Ye-es!' she says. 'Do you want to try anything? Waggle the gear stick about? Slot it in a few times?'

It occurs to me that this young lady is on the verge of employing techniques not usually practised by the average used car salesman. It also occurs to me that I am a sucker for such tactics. Below dashboard level, percy is responding to the warmth and the promise of good times ahead and is beginning to dent my denims.

'Are you sure it's all right?' I allow my digits to take a stroll along her left thigh. They meet nobody who tells them that they are trespassing.

'Oh yes. We want you to be completely satisfied with what you're getting.'

You can't say much fairer than that, can you? I don't know what sales manual this girl uses but she could go a long way.

Wasting no further time on idle chit chat, I lean across and show her how good I am at sealing envelopes. She snuggles closer and I draw her towards me and ease her over the hand-brake which separates the two seats. Her legs are now alongside mine and she thoughtfully props one of them against the clutch pedal. In this way there is much less danger of me damaging my wristwatch as I slide my mit up to say hello to her snatch-box. She is an eager little thing and her brewer's bung probes for my hairy goat like it is an escaping eel. She is wearing stockings like her sister and it is a real treat to glide from nylon to warm, soft flesh. There's not that feeling of being trapped at the end of a bag that you get with tights. I hook my finger under the rim of her knicks and she grabs hold of my balls like it is a game of Pass the Parcel and she reckons she is on to a winner.

'Let me get across you,' she says. Nothing bashful about her, is there? It's not a question of an hour and a half's foreplay and 'I'm sorry but I'm saving myself for the curate'. I have hardly got my zip open before she has wrenched my pants and jeans down to knee level. Percy bobs in front of me as if nodding his agreement to some unspoken – and probably unspeakable – suggestion and Suzanne raises her chassis and sheds her panties before you can say Roger Carpenter.

'Here we go then.' With an agility that suggests that she has done something not totally unlike this before, Suzanne slides a leg across my lap and lays one of her delicate little hands on my poke spoke. 'Say goodbye to daddy,' she murmurs. A quick wriggle and my friend has disappeared. Suzanne slides her arms round my neck and settles into a position from which any Rhode Island Red watching would expect her to hatch out my balls.

'What's your after sales service like?' I ask.

Suzanne bounces up and down and closes her eyes. I think her mind is on something else. 'Do you want me to do it faster?' she says.

The engine is still running and the heater is still on and I can't help feeling that it is getting a bit on the warm side. The condensation running down the inside of the windows is a big help in reaching this conclusion.

'That's lovely,' I say. I mean it, too. The sensation is like a butterfly's wings tickling a naked current – don't ask me how I know, I just do. Not wishing to interfere with anyone's pleasure, I sneak out a hand and try and find the heater control.

'Hold me.' Suzanne intercepts my hand and guides it to her back bumpers. She is now shaking about like a sack of warm jelly beans and it is clear to me that something explosive is about to happen. Quite what it is comes as something of a surprise.

Suzanne swings out one of her legs, there is a grinding noise – mechanical – and the lorry suddenly lurches forward. She must have knocked it into gear. Before I can take any rescue action I have been thrown back in my seat by the sudden movement and achieved some of the deepest penetration you will read about outside a sex instruction manual. The incident could not have taken place at a worse moment because I was just about to see off a few hundred thousand friends. Now I don't reckon that I could wave goodbye to my granny if you gave me a Union Jack on a couple of sticks. Down and out, percy dives for the shelter of my thighs and I fumble for the ignition. CRUNCH! We hit something and I slide across the seat with Suzanne still on top of me. She is screaming her head off and I can't say I blame her. We are still moving but I can't see where because of the steamed up windows.

Womp!! We hit something else and, more by luck than judgement, I bash against the gear lever and knock it into neutral. No sooner has the vehicle stopped than Suzanne has opened the door and started to clamber out. She does not even wait for her knicks. That is one big advantage that birds have in an emergency. There is no chance of a bloke scarpering with his trousers round his ankles.

We seem to have come to a halt with the snout of the lorry half way through the perimeter wire. It looks like something out of a prisoner of war movie. *The Great Escape* – you must have seen it. They have it on the telly every other Sunday. Behind us are a couple of bashed in motors that now have a bit more knocked off them than is indicated by the price reduction.

Sid steams up and it is soon clear that he has something on his mind beside a couple of inches of thinning barnet. 'You bleeding half wit!!' he screams. 'What do you think you're doing? I haven't paid for them yet.' I am disturbed to see that the idiot has what appears to be a bundle of five pound notes in his mit.

'We had a bit of an accident,' I say. 'Look, Sid. You're not seriously thinking of buying these crates, are you?'

'What about the damage?' chips in Babs, hoisting her

knicks towards waist level. 'That's going to cost a few bob to put right.'

'And my ankle,' says Suzanne. 'It's irreplaceable. I want retribution!'

'Now look what you've done!' snarls Sid. 'Everything going like clockwork and you have to cock it up! Gawd, I'd love to have you along at a peace conference.'

'Your flies are undone,' I tell him.

We called at Sid's place on the way to Battersea but I had no idea he was arming himself with a load of expensive moola. When he told me to wait in the car and went down the end of the garden I thought he had just remembered to feed the kid's ferrets – that tells you something about Sid, doesn't it? Most kids have rabbits. Sid's kids have ferrets. Mind you, when you look at the kids it is a wonder they don't have alligators. Jason and Jerome Noggett are about as lovable as a couple of tarantulas dyed baby pink.

'Daddykins isn't going to like this,' says Suzanne menacingly.

'No-er, well, let's see what we can work out.' Sid goes into a huddle with the ladies and I hear the crackle of fivers changing hands. It is funny but I would swear that I could smell ferrets. Maybe that is why Sid has his finger tied up with a piece of rag – or handkerchief as he prefers to call it.

Finally, the meeting breaks up. 'That'll do for now then,' says Babs. 'We'll go and see what Dad says, eh Suzanne? He's got your address, hasn't he?'

'Of course he has!' scolds my lovely partner. 'We all live together, don't we!?'

'Not you, you stupid cow!' says Babs pleasantly. 'I was talking to short arse, wasn't I?'

'What happened to Paul Newman?' I ask.

'Piss off!'

The girls scramble through the hole I have so thoughtfully made in the wire mesh and click-clack down the empty street.

'You berk!' snarls Sid. 'You cost me another hundred quid there.'

'It might be more,' I say, 'You could find their old man on your doorstep.'

'Not on my doorstep.' Sid looks smug. 'You don't think I gave him my real address, do you? Wake up, Timmo. You've got to think fast in this business: "Sting like a butterfly, dance like a bee." That's what they say, isn't it?'

'Something like that,' I say, wearily.

'I'm afraid that money will have to come out of your wages.'

'Wait a minute!' I say. 'I'm still employed by Slumbernog. Nitya Pullova is only half way through *The Boyhood of Lenin*. I reckon he's going to get his end away soon.'

'Is that all you can think about?' sneers Sid. 'Communist bedtime stories? Let me tell you something. Unless you join up with Nogget Transport, you're never going to earn enough money to pay me back.'

'I'll think about it,' I say.

'You do that. Now, come on, let's get the fleet out of here.'

'Fleet'. It is almost touching, isn't it? Sid is just like a big, soft kid with a new toy. Unless I can get him fixed up with a nursemaid I don't see how I can leave him to fend for himself.

'How are we going to get them out?' I ask.

'Through that bleeding hole you made. Come on!'

I have just climbed into the cab and turned on the lights – or rather, light, as it turns out to be – when the door is wrenched open and a mean looking cove is revealed grasping a spanner.

'Right!' he says. 'One little move and I'll smash your ankle into matchwood. Alf! Get the rossers.'

'Hang on a minute,' I say. 'What are you raving about?'

'You're trying to nick these lorries, aren't you?'

'Nick them?! My mate's just bought them!'

'Don't give me that. I'd have known if he'd have bought them, wouldn't I?'

'I don't see why,' I say. 'He only did it five minutes ago.'

'I'd have known because I own them!' shouts the bloke. 'I'm Harry Trenchmouth. I own Squaredeal Cars.'

While his words are burning their way into the innermost recesses of my lugholes their significance is moving at an even faster pace. Unless I am very much mistaken, Sid has been taken to the cleaners again. I thought there was something too good to be true about that Rogers bloke. And Babs and Suzanne did not come over like anyone's daughters. No wonder my little charmer was puzzled when I started rabbiting about Australia. I don't expect that anyone had told her about that.

'I think there's been some mistake,' I say 'My brother-in-law will be able to explain everything.'

As if on cue, another villainous herbert appears prodding Sid at the end of an iron bar. 'You hold them here, Alf,' says Mr T. 'I'll phone for the police. If they try anything, don't hesitate to bash them repeatedly with your winkle pin.'

'You must listen to me!' whines Sid. 'We were conned. We bought these vehicles in good faith. I had no idea the people who sold them to us weren't the rightful owners.'

'You expect me to believe that?!' says Mr Trenchmouth, scornfully. 'I catch you red-handed, absconding with the vehicles through a hole you have clearly made for that very purpose, and you have the bare-faced cheek to say that you have purchased the aforementioned vehicles in the course of a normal business transaction. Do you expect anyone in their right senses to believe a story like that? Alf, give him a little tap for being naughty.'

'Hang on a minute!' says Sid, taking a fast step backwards. 'Don't call the fuzz. Maybe we can come to some arrangement.'

'What kind of arrangement?' says Mr T suspiciously.

'You want to sell these lorries, don't you?'

'They're not here for decoration,' says Mr T.

'Well,' says Sid, wringing his hands nervously. 'To save a lot of awkwardness, I'll buy them from you – of course, I've already bought them once but I can understand your not believing that.'

Mr T looks at Sid and shakes his head. 'Did you hear that, Alf? He's offering me a bribe not to turn him in. He's trying to corrupt the course of justice.'

'That's not true!' yelps Sid. 'I'm just trying to do what's best.'

'What's best for *you*,' says Trenchmouth.

'What's best for all of us!' says Sid.

'I'd be breaking the law if I didn't hand you over,' says Mr T. There is a slight waver in his voice and Sid leaps in desperately.

'I'd make it worth your while,' he says.

'There's a lot of damage to the site, guvnor,' chips in Alf. 'I reckon the Ford's a write-off.'

'To say nothing of what you've done to the fencing,' muses Trenchmouth. 'No, we'll have to do our duty, Alf. I wouldn't let these two out of my sight, anyway.'

'I've got cash,' says Sid. A bundle of notes leaps into his Margates, and Trenchmouth's minces open wide.

'Did you pull a bank before you came round here?' he says.

'My life savings,' said Sid, pathetically.

Ten minutes later, the bulge in Mr Trenchmouth's jacket looks like a pregnant moggy and Sid is set to start saving all over again.

'Right,' says the fortunate owner of Squaredeal Motors. 'I still think I may have done the wrong thing. This incident could haunt me for the rest of my life.'

'It's certainly going to haunt me,' mutters Sid.

'Let my soft heart be a warning to you,' says Mr T. 'Tread ye the ways of righteousness and honesty for the rest of your days.'

'Amen,' says Alf.

With that, they step into an XK 120 and are away. 'Phew!' says Sid. 'It took all my fast talking to get us out of that one, didn't it?'

'That and a few million quid,' I say. 'Blimey! How much money have you got?'

'Practically sweet FA after that lot,' says Sid. 'Come on, let's get out of here before something else happens.'

It is now about one o'clock in the morning and I am really knackered. It is amazing how a few beers with Sid can stretch into half a life time of incident. I drag myself into the cabin, tap the gear stick and feel for the ignition. It would be just my luck if the bastard did not start. Vroom! Thank God for that. I find first gear, ease out the clutch and slowly crawl forward with the wire mesh scraping against the side panels.

Ringa-ding-ding-ding-ding-ding-ring-ring-!!! At first, I think it is a fire engine. Then I cop an eyeful of the flashing blue light. The fuzz! What a night this is turning out to be. I hope they are not going to keep us hanging about with a lot of damn fool questions.

'OK. Turn off the motor and get out!' The bule is standing beside me almost before the door of his Panda car has slammed. I don't mess about but do as he says.

As usual, Sid has got more to say. 'What is the meaning of this, officer? Can't an innocent man go about his business without being hounded by the forces of the law?'

Before any answer can be given to this interesting question a tiny geezer in a camel hair overcoat bristles before Sid like a balding Yorkshire terrier.

'Bring back the birch!' he screams. 'It's the only thing these swine understand.'

Sid turns to the copper. 'Would you mind asking Tiny Tim to step out of the way of my lorry? Otherwise he might land up wedged in one of the treads.'

The bule fixes Sid with a beady eye. '*Your* lorry? That's very interesting. This is Mr Deal of Squaredeal Motors and he says that it's *his* lorry.'

CHAPTER THREE

In which Timmy's firm young body is cruelly used by Noreen and Avril while our hero attempts to bring Bango fish to the Hai Bali Tabernacle.

'You should never have hit that copper,' I say.

'I'd had enough,' says Sid. 'I was overcome, distraught. In the circumstances, it was a very normal thing to do. Anyway, there was something funny about him.'

'Yeah, he was a black belt judo expert.'

'I didn't mean that,' says Sid, massaging the back of his neck. 'I meant something funny about the way he behaved. I was dead certain he was an impostor. Did you see his feet?'

I nod. 'I did catch a glimpse of them when he was standing on your chest.'

'They weren't like copper's feet. More like a bleeding ballet dancer.'

'Well, aren't you the lucky one,' I tell him. 'It might have been Jack Warner.'

'It's a blooming disgrace,' grumbles Sid. 'When I was a kiddy, a copper looked like a copper. You could hear him coming a mile off. Now, they trip around like a load of fairies.'

'It's a pity you didn't suss out that some of those other geezers were impostors, isn't it?' I tell him.

Sid adopts his martyred expression. 'Im not ashamed to have faith in my fellow men. If we all went round wearing a black mask of suspicion, where would we be?'

'I don't know where we'd be,' I say. 'But I know, wherever it was, we'd be a lot richer.'

'That's right, that's right,' says Sid, bitterly, 'Always ready with the cheap gag. It's easy, isn't it?'

'I'm sorry Sid,' I say. 'But it was a bit – how shall I put it? – unfortunate. If you hadn't bought all those tickets for the Policeman's Ball we might have ended up in the chokey.'

'You didn't help by thinking it was a raffle,' snarls Sid. 'I thought that bloke was going to charge us when you asked what they were going to do with the other half of the set.' We are standing beside the lorries which are now parked outside the ancestral home of the Leas in Scraggs Lane. Sid eventually bought them from Mr Deal who by some miracle turned out to actually own them. Sid – very understandably – keeps pretty quiet about the details but I am led to understand that he could have bought two new lorries for what he ended up laying out in the three transactions. Needless to say, Will Rogers, Harry Trenchmouth, Alf, Babs and Suzanne have not been seen since. I reckon they are probably drinking Sid's health in the South of France.

Sid shapes as if to give one of the lorries a cheerful slap and then thinks better of it. 'Right,' he says. 'That's all behind us now – as the snake said when the doctor told him he had piles.' Sid waits hopefully and I run a bit of bird shit off what remains of the paintwork. 'You've no sense of humour, have you?' he says bitterly.

'I think it's spending so much time with you,' I say. 'What have you got lined up for us now, stock car racing? or straight round to the scrap metal yard?'

'Sarcasm is the lowest form of wit, Einstein,' sneers Sid. 'While you've been looking on the black side. I've been doing something positive. I've lined you up with a nice little number already.'

'What are you on about?' I tell him.

'I'm still employed by Slumbernog.'

'No you're not,' says Sid. 'I rang up the acting shop steward and told him that you thought the TUC were a bunch of pricks. I wouldn't go back there for a few years if I were you.'

'You rotten sod!' I say. 'Now I'll never know what happened to Vladimir Ilyich when he returned from exile.'

'And a good thing too!' says Sid. 'That Russian tart was poisoning your mind with her big tits.'

Sid may say what he likes but I will always have a soft spot for the fair maid of Omsk. I only wish that Nitya Pullova had been prepared to repay the compliment.

'All right,' I say. 'What is it? I suppose I should be touched that you realise you can't get on without me.'

'That's it,' soothes Sid. 'I try to appear hard but basically I'm a bundle of sentiment. What used to be purely a business relationship has grown into something deeper and far more fulfilling – give us a kiss!'

'Get off me!' I shout. 'Stop messing about and tell me what you want me to do.'

'Dead simple. Just a little doddle to start with. Pick up a consignment from the docks and tool up the M1 to the Hai Bali Tabernacle at Nuneaton.'

'The Hai Bali Tabernacle?' I say.

'Yeah, they're a load of religious freaks. Very nice but a bit round the bend. They're health food nuts and all that caper.'

'So what am I taking up there, Sid?'

'I believe it's very nice. Some geezer left them his country seat. Nobody would do that for me. They wouldn't even leave me what dropped out of it.'

'What's the load, Sid?'

'You won't have any trouble finding it. Just turn off at—'

'Sid, stop beating about the twat fuzz! What am I carrying?'

'Fish,' says Sid.

'Fish? I thought you said they were on a health food kick. They don't eat fish, do they?'

'They don't eat fish that's been caught,' says Sid.

'Blimey! You're not saying that this lot gave itself up, are you?'

'In a manner of speaking,' says Sid. 'It's the Bango fish, you see. The Bango fish is like a lemming.'

'You mean it's round and yellow?'

'A lemming, not a lemon, you berk! Lemmings have the death wish, don't they? They dive off cliffs and swim out to sea until they snuff it. The Bango fish is the opposite. It jumps out of the water and lies there waiting to be picked up.'

'Like Natalie Perkins down at Streatham Baths,'

'Exactly. Only I believe there's a bit more flesh on the Bango fish.'

'What a remarkable creature, Sid.'

'I've never tried it, Timmo. Mind you, I have heard a few things. That bloke who bottled Don Tidworth had a go and was very favourably impressed.'

'Liked the taste, did he?'

Sid looks shocked. 'I didn't ask for the details. Blimey! You are a dirty little sod, aren't you?'

'I was talking about the Bango fish, Sid – not Natalie Perkins! ! I was making reference to life's rich tapestry, its lights and shades, the ever-varying—'

'All right, all right! If I want to know the rest I'll buy the book. Now, stop farting about and get down to the docks. There's no time to lose.'

When I get down to the docks, I see what Sid means. He forgot to tell me that there had been a strike. The niff is worse than a marathon dancer's nylon socks after a jitterbug session. The crates of fish don't have to be loaded on to the back of the lorry, they hop up by themselves.

'You'd better drive fast, mate,' says one of the dockers. 'If the pong catches up with you, you'll be a gonner.'

He is not kidding. At the first traffic lights, the bloke next to me falls off his motor bike. It must be bad because when I have to stop outside a fishmonger's, one of the kippers folds up and touches its toes.

I am just approaching the M1 when I see the bird. She has shoulder length hair and a sheepskin coat that is browsing round her ankles. A leg protrudes temptingly from the front of the coat and the eye can travel about twelve inches above the knee without bumping into any sign of a skirt. It is a journey that is very easy to make. As I swing dangerously near to the curb, the bird brushes some hair from her eyes and rolls a lazy thumb skywards.

The lorry has very good brakes. Much better, for instance, than the Morris 1100 that is right behind me. Of course, the bloke at the wheel might have been clocking the bird, as well. I do suggest this but he seems to take great exception to the idea. Possibly because of the reaction of the old boiler sitting next to him. You could lose all interest with her about.

Of course, by the time I have got the bloke's bonnet out from underneath my back number plate, the bird has been picked up by some other lucky sod. It's tragic, really. I could sense that we were made for each other. You know how you can, sometimes. 'Laura, on the train that is passing through' – though not while it is in the station, of course. The bloke who has run into me even tries to say that it is my fault but I am not having any of that. I know my rights. In the end it is the fish that get me out of it. The bloke's old lady is so pissed off with the pong that she tells him to forget about me and get the hell out of it. I can't say I blame her, I wish I could do the same.

I get on the motorway and it is all very uneventful. Mile after mile with nothing to do but think about things that never come into your mind. When, and if, Sid ever gives me any moola I will have to buy a wireless.

It is not long before I start feeling like a cuppa and by the time we get to the Supercon complex of restaurants and filling stations my tongue is hanging down the front of my shirt – It makes a change from wearing a tie.

I feel like a leak so I peel off and follow the sign that says 'Gents'. By the cringe! What a dump. I was not expecting a bloke in a white jacket to hand me a towel but when you look at the wall you expect to see 'fuck' spelled properly, don't you? I mean 'fuk' just isn't good enough with the amount we spend on comprehensive education. I don't begrudge paying the taxes but I do expect to get a little more for my money. I would not mind getting a towel, either. I know that there must have been soap here once because I can see the two little metal arms that used to hold the dispenser. The Towelomat looks like a tin of sardines that somebody tried to kick open when the opener bust – they always do, don't they? I am glad I don't want to do anything more creative than a slash because the inside of the cubicle that I am looking at – it is very easy to look inside because the only thing that remains of the doors is the hinges – reminds me of a lost property office for turds. As for the niff – well, I feel like rushing out and taking a lungful of Bango fish.

The cafeteria isn't a big improvement. The strongest thing about the tea is the taste of the paper cup and the smell of grease makes me think that they must have just boiled a channel swimmer. If they did, they definitely served up his flippers in the sandwich I am eating. I am wondering why someone wanted to dip the sugar sprinkler in his tea so that the holes clogged up when I see the bird I was about to fall in love with earlier. She is sitting very erect with her hands cupped round her teacup and an expression of complete boredom on her mug. I try and smile at her and she looks through me like I am the invisible man. Obviously, nobody has told her about my magnetism. I must do something about that. I am very partial to birds who treat me like an attack of cystitis on their wedding night because I admire their taste. I reckon that anybody who laps me up must be desperate, and who wants to go about with desperate birds?

The bird sips her tea slowly and closes her eyes. One of the things I like about her most of all is that she does not seem to be with anyone. The bloke who gave her a lift must have pushed on. Either that or he tried to get fresh and copped a smack in the kisser, or – even more exciting possibility – got what he wanted and then pushed on. I wonder if she does? She must do. She looks very experienced. When you get close you can see that she wears a lot of eye make-up and that clinches it, doesn't it? I mean, once they start wanging about with the old eye pencil they're writing 'I want it' all round their mince pies.

I knock back my cha like it is a couple of fingers of rye and start to mosey towards her table. For one thing the tea is diabolical and for another, you can't let a thing like that lie about and expect to find it when you want it. She doesn't look up as I come towards her which is just as well because it means that she doesn't see me barge into one of the tables and get sworn at by a bloody great navvy with his jaws locked round a bacon sandwich. I leave him to pour his tea back into the cup and prepare to make with the verbal fireworks. There was a time when I was tongue-tied with birds but now the chat just pours out. The secret is to practise what you are going to say first so that you don't have any of that awkward mumbling – mind you, it is best to do it with your mouth firmly shut. One bird told me she nearly gave me the brush because she saw my lips moving as I came towards her and thought I had some kind of nervous tic.

'Hi,' I say. 'Is anybody sitting here?' The delivery is faultless. I hit all my stresses and I sound so relaxed and friendly that for a moment I think it is someone else talking.

'Yes.'

This in an answer I am not prepared for. 'Oh,' I say. 'Yes, well-um, er, yes.' It would be a good idea if you could practise the second thing you say as well. 'Er – I can't see anybody.'

The bird half rises to her feet and leans across the table so that she is looking down onto the seat opposite. She stares at it for a moment. 'You're right. They must be in the toilet.'

It occurs to me that she is taking the mickey. 'I thought you might want a lift,' I say. 'Pardon me for breathing.'

'That's all right, but don't make a habit of it.' The lady speaks with a brummy accent and is clearly a comedienne.

'Do you mind if I sit down till your friend comes back?'

'You already have.'

'Would you like a cup of tea or something?'

'No thanks.'

'Where are you heading for?'

'Anywhere.'

'I'm going to Nuneaton.'

'All right, let's go.' The bird stands up and looks at me expectantly.

'What about your friend?'

'Fook him.'

'Oh-er, yes, all right.' It occurs to me that this bird has a very variable temperament. I know it is a woman's something or other to change her mind but you don't usually come across bints who put the idea into practice with such relish.

We walk across the restaurant and everybody is looking at us. She really is a knockout bird, this one. I then notice that there is a long strip of toilet paper unwinding behind us. It is coming from underneath her coat.

'You a soccer fan, are you?' I say.

'What do you mean?' She looks down and her features huddle together for an instant. 'Booger!' She feels inside her coat and pulls at something. The toilet paper streamer flutters to the ground and a plastic ashtray clatters across the floor. I move decisively towards the door. Something tells me that the lady may have light-fingered tendencies.

'What's your name?' I say.

'I don't have one.'

I push open the reinforced glass door with what appears to be bullet holes in it. 'You must have.'

The bird pulls her coat around her and looks up at the front of the building. 'Supercon,' she says in a take it or leave it voice. I don't think it is her name.

I start walking towards the lorry park. 'You haven't got a car, then?' she says.

'Not with me.'

'I was talking about now,' she says sarcastically. 'Have you got a wireless?'

'Not yet.'

She shakes her head, sadly. 'Some booger nicked my tranny.'

'You have to be careful,' I say.

We are not exactly racing forward with the speed of a forest fire words-wise but I don't reckon that Cary Grant would make a lot of headway with his bird.

'Pooh! !' she says. 'Do you smell that?'

'Bango fish,' I say. 'They're very interesting. They dive out of the water and nut themseves.'

'If I smelt like that I'd nut myself,' says the lady. 'Is that what you've got?' She makes it sound like the measles.

'I'm taking them up to the Hai Bali Tabernacle at Nuneaton,' I explain. 'They can't eat flesh that has been killed for the table but these fish are all right because they've done themselves in. Fascinating, isn't it?'

If the lady agrees with me she is not at pains to reveal the fact. 'Urgh! !' she says. 'I'm not travelling with them. I'd throw up.'

'You soon get used to it,' I say. 'Once we start moving you won't know they're there.'

'Don't make me laugh. You've got a bleeding cheek expecting anyone to travel with a load of rotting fish!'

'Having trouble, Shirl?' The speaker is leaning out of the cab of a twenty ton truck and has a wallpaper of tattoos all the way up a forearm that looks like weight lifter's thigh.

'This daft booger's messing me about.'

'Well, hop up here, then.'

'Where are you going?'

'Come up here and you'll find out.'

'Piss off!'

'Right.' The lorry begins to ease forward.

'Hang on a minute!'

The bird disappears round the front of the truck without

a glance in my direction and I see the driver lean across to open the door. Seconds later, his bonce juts out of the cab and he winks at me. 'Ta rar, lad.' There is a squeak from the air brakes and the monster motor swalches across the tarmac and points its blunt nose towards London. Exit another great romance. Something about the bloke and his lorry makes me feel insignificant. I am like the bloke in the Charles Atlas advertisements who gets the sand kicked in his mush. I feel like Wee Georgie Wood standing next to Cassius Clay in the shower. What you might call a percy-cution complex. It is all very sad because I had reckoned that the life of a long distance lorry driver would be a regular nooky fest. Oggins mad crumpet lining the highway so to speak. Apart from Shirl, or whatever her name was, Supercon was very short on unaccompanied frippet. Come to think of it, it was very short on lorry drivers too. Not surprising when you consider the fare provided. I will have to reserve my judgement until I hit a real honest-to-goodness transport caff.

Slightly cheered, I brace my nostrils and return to Enid – this being what I have decided to call my crate. There is something prim and dignified about the name that suits the old rust cart down to the valve caps. It may not be the fastest thing on the road but it does have a kind of battered class.

The rest of my journey till I turn off the motorway is uneventful. Perhaps urged on by the pong behind her, Enid chugs along at a solid fifty-five mph and I begin to turn my mind to the scene that awaits me at the Hai Bali Tabernacle. I have always had the feeling that these 'alternative society' set-ups are no more than an excuse for an unlimited ration of in and out and I will be interested to see whether there are patches of flattened grass all round the parkland.

There is a sign soon after I leave the motorway and a mile later a crumbling red brick wall shuts off my view of the first few feet of rolling grassland peppered with clumps of tall trees. This must be the place. Another couple of miles and I come to the gatehouse. There is a metal pole barring the entrance and an officious looking geezer springs into view as I shove on the anchors. He has a mouth as tight as the washer on a three inch screw and eyebrows like cigarette burns on a plastic work surface.

'Down here!' He jerks a thumb towards the ground at his feet and it takes me a second to realise that he is not drawing my attention to a dog turd. This is not quite the welcome I was expecting but I suppose I had better show willing. It is my first job and I don't want there to be any slip ups. I switch the engine off and climb out of the cab.

'Right! Everything off.'

Blimey! If he expects me to strip down to the buff in this weather he has got another think coming. Blooming nudists! I don't mind them wandering about starkers. Why should they grumble if I wear clothes? Still, like I said, I don't want any trouble. Probably best to do like the man says.

'What the heck do you think you're doing?!'

'I'm taking my clothes off,' I say, lowering my trousers to knee level.

'I meant, everything off the back of the lorry, you fool!'

The bloke clearly has no sense of humour. It is quite a humorous misunderstanding when you think about it, isn't it? No? Oh well, please yourselves.

'You want me to deliver it here?'

'No! I want to check your vehicle.'

'It's only Bango fish,' I say.

Stoat-features starts to walk round to the back of the lorry. 'The make of fertiliser is immaterial,' he says. 'It's what you might be trying to smuggle in with it.'

What a funny man. I am about to ask him for further details when I fall over – I have forgotten about the position of my trousers.

When I stand up, the gatekeeper is recoiling from the back of the lorry with a handkerchief held to his hooter. 'Urgh! It's disgusting!' he croaks. 'Get it round to the home farm immediately.'

'You don't want to search it, then?'

'Get out of it!'

The bloke is turning the colour of green blotting paper. Either he is very sensitive or my bracket must be getting used to the niff.

'That's a nice uniform,' I say. 'Do they make it in your size?'

The bloke does not say anything but waves me on my way with a sign presumably meant to tell me that the turning to Home Farm is two hundred yards up the road. In fact it is nearer half a mile before the road forks and I see a collection of farm buildings huddled together near open fields. Quite why they want the fish here, I don't know. Maybe they mix them up with potatoes to make some kind of fishcake. There are certainly a lot of spuds about. In one of the fields, a tractor is ploughing up thousands of the bastards and a gang of bints is following on behind loading them into sacks. One little darling takes a shufti at me and in no time they are all whistling and shouting. It is surprising really. I mean, I know I am fascinating and all that but you would think that they would be up to the thigh-balls with fellas. I give them a relaxed wave, narrowly avoid driving into a ditch, and pull up behind a row of tin shacks. There does not seem to be anyone about so I climb out of the cab and – 'Psssst!!'

Somebody is trying to attract my attention from a half-opened doorway. I cross the yard and detect the not unfamiliar outline of a bird beckoning to me from the shadows.

'Come here!' The urgency in her voice surprises me.

'I've brought the Bangos,' I say, wondering why I am lowering my voice.

'In here!' she hisses.

I don't argue with her but go into the shed. There are potatoes everywhere – well, not quite everywhere. Some of the room is taken up by a couple of birds. They are smoking snouts and wearing wellington boots, jeans and anoraks. Despite that, they look not unappealing. Especially the larger one. She reminds me of Silvana Bigknockers or whatever that earthy Italian bird was called. I remember seeing her in a season of continental films they had on at the Classic, Tooting. In every one of them she was standing up to her generation gap in the rice fields and getting gang banged by half a dozen blokes on a bit of wasteland behind a large block of flats. The films were pretty boring really, though I don't think the subtitles helped. I mean, she was never saying 'Be careful of my religious relics' when the big geezer humped her through the wall of the shack.

'You're new, aren't you?' says the smaller one of the two birds.

'Sort of,' I say. 'I haven't done this before.'

The birds look at each other. 'Really?'

'That's right,' I say. 'Where do you want it?'

The big bird stubs out her cigarette and blows the smoke out of her mouth like she can't wait to get rid of it. 'No need to rush it, ducks. We're desperate, but not that desperate. What's your name?'

'Timmy Lea.'

'I'm Noreen and this is Avril.'

'That's French for April,' says the smaller charmer, helpfully.

I consider the ways in which this piece of information could change my life and make with the introductory nod. 'You all muck in together, do you?' I ask looking round at the shelves of potatoes presumably laid out to dry.

'We take it in turns to slip off,' says Noreen. 'Anyway, there's never enough fellas for a team scene.' While I digest this remark she starts running her hand up my arm and fondling my biceps – yes, I do have them. 'And you've never done it before,' she says with a sense of wonder invading her voice. 'Well, that will make a change.'

'I've always wanted to initiate a young boy,' says Avril.

'I've always wanted to be able to pronounce "initiate",' says Noreen.

With these words, she buries her head in my shoulder and sinks her Teds into my bushel. Quite amazing behaviour, I am certain you will agree! And it is not only her fangs that are dishing out the aggression. Her left hand runs over my action man kit like it is trying to use it as Polyfilla to block up the crack between my thighs.

'What about the Bangos?' I say desperately.

'All in good time, you cock-happy son of the sod!' With these confusing words, Avril launches herself on to my cakehole and steals a march on Noreen's fingers by sliding her mit down the inside of my trousers. Percy is not slow to notice that living conditions are becoming crowded and lunges upwards. The girls grab for him like he is an escaped bar of soap.

It is becoming evident to me that, in many respects, the behaviour of these two bints is much different to that which you would expect to find at the average royal investiture or vicar's induction ceremony. A certain frenzy characterises their actions and seems at odds with my impression of the Hai Bali Tabernacle as being a reservoir of sexual freedom. Those birds don't appear to have tasted the fruit of the Y-front in many a long day.

'Me first!'

'No, me!'

Their combined weight pushes me behind a pile of potato-filled sacks and I find myself sinking floorwards into a nest of sacking clearly arranged for an occasion such as the one which – with any luck – is about to take place.

'Give me a hand with my wellies.'

'Only if I can go first.'

'All right, greedy guts!'

Noreen lies down beside me and Avril tugs off her boots and wipes her muddy hands on the nearest sack.

I have seen some unveiling ceremonies in my time but the speed with which Noreen sheds her slacks is a natural for the *Guinness Book of Records*. What a pity Ross and Truss aren't interested in things like that.

'Right, ducks,' says Noreen, lying back and smoothing her hands over her thighs. 'Come on, there's nothing to be frightened of.'

'I'm not frightened,' I say.

Noreen cocks her head to one side as I head my cock to the other. 'No, I can see you're not,' she says.

I can't help wishing that she would take her anorak off but the way things are rushing along it is obvious that a few of the refinements are going to have to be dispensed with.

'Come between my legs,' she says.

Immediately there is a squeak of protest from Avril. 'Don't put ideas in his head!'

'I mean, kneel between my legs. That's right, now—'

'Like this?' I say innocently.

'That's right. Very good!'

'Beginner's luck – oops! Sorry.'

'Oh no!' says Avril. 'Don't say he's—'

'It slipped out,' says Noreen. 'Do stop jumping up and down. You'll spoil it for everyone. Come on, Timmy, you're a right little riveter. Isn't he doing well, Avril?'

'Amazing,' says Avril. 'He's taken to it like a dick to water.'

'I suppose it is a natural instinct,' says Noreen. 'Oooh! That is nice.'

I tune out their voices and abandon myself to enjoying the strawberry ripples that are yo-yoing down to my toes and back again, each one bouncing higher so that I can eventually deflect them from my shoulder blades down to my kneading finger tips. Noreen's back bollocks are willowing through my fingers like a couple of understuffed cushions and I try and concentrate them into a tighter target for my funny gun.

Avril has now shed her threads and crept up behind me. Whilst I deliver my message of good cheer to Noreen's nether regions her saucy fingers collide with my cobblers and start ringing a graceful peal or two. Sensitive readers will be glad to learn that the skills learned in the potato fields are not easily transmitted to the amorous couch and that there is no danger of my knackers joining the pile of King Edwards over her left shoulder. Noreen, however, is obviously sensitive about sharing her toys.

'Stop messing him about!' she scolds.

'Oh, do give over! He likes it, don't you, love?'

'Not bad,' I say. The bird clearly does not spend a fortune on hand cream but I have known worse.

'He's only saying that to be polite,' says Noreen.

'It's my turn, anyway,' says Avril. 'Let him go. You've had quite long enough.'

'Oh no I haven't,' says Noreen, kicking one of her gumboots out of the way. 'Some of us are sensitive. I can't be turned on like a tap. I have to be wooed.'

'What you're doing now is rude,' says Avril.

While the girls continue their argument I decide that it is time to stamp my personality on the proceedings. Unless I start to sort Noreen out I am going to be stuck on this pile of sacks till the cows come home – and you can imagine how nasty that could be. Crushing the lusty lady to me like she is a roll of carpet I am carrying up a steep flight of stairs, I proceed to pulverise her with my pelvis until a railway enthusiast would expect to see steam coming out of her navel and the two of us chugging off towards New Street Station. She begins to shudder like a small vessel about to break up in a heavy sea and I brace myself for the warning note of orgasmic yodel. I am always in danger of unloading myself when a bird starts her sperm wail and it occurs to me that, with Avril literally breathing down my neck, this would be a bad moment to lose my deposit. Today of all days, I don't want to disappoint anybody. If the members of the Hai Bali Tabernacle like to keep themselves to themselves behind guarded gates and enjoy screwing visiting deliverymen then that is their affair. I am not here to pass moral judgements.

Thinking hard of hob-nailed boots and Anthony Wedgwood Benn's chest expander I weather out the storm that is now raging beneath me. Noreen is so carried away that she has clawed her way into the sacks of potatoes stacked behind her and is throwing handfuls of spuds against the corrugated iron walls of the shed.

'Have you left anything for me?' Noreen does not reply to Avril's self-interested question so the next candidate for my jolly lolly turns hopefully to the man himself. 'Are you all right, love?'

I declutch from Noreen's crutch and Avril's greedy eyes

plunder my loins. 'Not bad,' I breathe modestly.

'Just lie back,' says Avril gratefully. 'I'll do all the work.'

Before I can say ta she has hopped across my hips and is slotting away my pork bayonet like she fears it might catch cold if left out in the open for too long. She places both her hands on my chest and begins to rock backwards and forwards making soft cooing noises.

'That's nice,' I say, indulging in a spot of pancake tossing with my thighs.

'He's getting the hang of it, fast, isn't he?' says Avril. Quite why these birds think that I am a stranger to pally alley I do not know but it is not a feature of our relationship that is going to worry me overmuch.

'Yes,' says Noreen looking down at me thoughtfully. 'I think he's ready for the next lesson, don't you? How would you like to try a love yodel, ducks?'

Before I have had time to consider fully what kind of vocal treat this quaintly named pursuit might entail there is the sound of jostling bodies approaching with no little haste. I tilt my head back to see half a dozen tousled birds peering over the sacks at us.

'Anything left?' says one of them.

'Push off!' snaps Avril. 'It's our turn. Get back to the field or you'll have the screws round here.'

The screws? The phrase is not unknown to me as anybody who has shared my experiences in one of Her Majesty's Prisons – or had any of their own – will know. (See *Confessions from the Clink* for harrowing details.) A screw is a warder. Why should they have warders at the Hai Bali Tabernacle?

'He's new, isn't he?' says another of the newcomers.

'Go away! You'll frighten him.' Avril pumps her hips up and down a few times as if keeping pace with a slow leak in a lilo.

'There's no harm in us watching.'

'Why don't you go and harvest a few turnips?' says Noreen cattily. 'I want to show Timmy how to pamper pussy.' She bends her eyes on me. 'The lap of the gods it's called, ducky.'

She scrambles on to my chest and I begin to feel like a dugout canoe with Avril controlling the rudder arrangement. Noreen wriggles forward and presses her knees down on my shoulder blades. There seems to be no doubt about it: I am in for a muff-mugging – ah well, worse things happen at sea.

'What's going on here? How many times do I have to tell you girls about smoking in here? You take a break when I tell you—'

'Good afternoon,' I say. The face is upside down but I can recognise it as belonging to a man wearing a military style peaked cap. I can also recognise it as wearing a very puzzled expression.

'What do you think you're doing?' says the face.

'I'm delivering the Bangos,' I say.

The face turns scarlet. 'Get off that man, Noakes!'

Noreen clambers off my chest. 'I was only trying to hold him down in case he turned ugly,' she says meekly.

'Don't give me that! I know what you were up to. Alderton!! Stop it this instant!' Avril has closed her eyes and sucked in her lower lip like she is trying to swallow her chin. While the man in the peaked cap bellows, she ricochets up and down on my action man kit like she is trying to light a fire with it. It is all highly confusing but, as the poet says, if you can't lick them, join them. I clench my minces and let the vats of warm honey flow over me –

'AAAAAAAAAAAAAAAAAAAAARGH!!!'

'Stop it, you disgusting little animals!' Peak cap tries to get to us round the sacks of potatoes but the girls get in his way and Noreen tips his hat over his eyes. By the time he has fought his way free, the worst – or more like, the best – is over. Avril shivers above me like the sail of a clipper that has been caught in a squall and I feel percy sinking earthwards like a kid that has banged the door-knocker a couple of times and is making a bunk for it round the corner.

'Get off him!!' Peak cap yanks Avril to her feet nearly taking me with her. There is a sympathetic gasp from those standing about us and a yelp from someone who is no longer standing – me.

'Why don't you mind your own business?!' I say. I always feel a bit grumpy after a spot of in and out, don't you?

Peak cap looks meaner than a Sid Nogget tip. 'You watch it!' he says. 'I'll have you put away.'

'I've just been put away,' I tell him. 'Listen, this is Hai Bali, isn't it?'

'High barley!?' says the bloke. 'These are potatoes.'

'I mean the Hai Barley Tabernacle,' I explain patiently. Honestly, it is amazing how stupid people can be, isn't it?

'Are you trying to be funny?' says the bloke. 'That's down the road. This is The Count Moriarty Country Home for Girls in Need of Care and Protection.' He leans towards me menacingly. 'In need of care and protection from scum like you! I saw what you were doing! Teaching these susceptible girls acts of shameless immorality. Pandering to the whims of their sensation-crazed bodies.' He starts fumbling with the buttons of his tunic. 'Supposing we all gave way to our natural impulses?' – there are murmurs of 'Right on!' and 'Let it all hang out, Big Daddy!' – 'Where would we be then? It would be disgusting, wouldn't it? Fannyfuckingtastic but disgusting!' so saying, he tears off his shirt and tunic and pulls down his trousers to gaiter level. He is still wearing a pair of long johns but this seems likely to be a temporary state of affairs as a wave of girls bears him floorwards.

What a carry-on! It does seem that I have made a foolish error. There was a big sign by the gate but I did not bother to look at it. Oh, foolish Timothy. Fortunately, all is not lost. I will recover my composure and my vehicle and flash round to the Hai Bali Whatsits. I hope they are not in the mood for any hai jinks because I feel that I have donated enough for one day.

I cross to the door and peer out. Enid is there but – oh no!! On the back of the lorry sits a confused tumble of empty boxes. What has happened to the Bango fish? I gaze out to the open fields and see a tractor drawing a contraption which is spraying some substance over the freshly ploughed earth. Some substance that has a particularly strong and familiar smell. What was it the man on the gate said? Fertiliser? Oh no! Sid is going to do his nut! What am I going to tell him?

'Would you like to come inside again?'

The bird at my elbow is small and wicked with eyes that glow like coals in the heart of a furnace. Her blouse is open to her navel and there is a smudge of dried earth pointing downwards from the cleft between her snow white breasts. She has a damp curl peeping over the edge of one of her ears and I tuck it out of sight while considering what to do. Possibly, I should go and see the people at the Hai Bali Tabernacle and tell them that the Bango fish were a bit far gone anyway. Maybe I should ring Sid. Either way there is not a lot of cause for urgent action. I turn away from the flock of gulls throwing up behind the tractor and close the door of the shed.

'Come and help me find my Y-fronts,' I say.

CHAPTER FOUR

In which Timmy has an accident and becomes heavily involved with Gladys, the elephant lady.

'You should never have taken delivery of them,' says Sid. 'Now I'm responsible for the cost to the Hai Bali geezers. None-eaten, that's appropriate, isn't it?'

'Yes, Sid. Very good,' I say.

'It's not very good! It's bleeding awful!!' screeched my highly strung brother-in-law.

'Now then, Sidney. You're not in your own home now, you know.'

That is Dad speaking. Nature's over-time ban. The only man who has been known to fall asleep with his hand on the lever of the clocking-in machine.

'Fancy a nice kipper fillet?' says Mum.

I suppress a shudder. 'No thanks, Mum. I'm a bit off fish at the moment.'

'They're blooming tough,' grumbles Dad, scraping his knife backwards and forwards across the plate.

'You haven't taken the cellophane off them,' says Mum.

'You're supposed to take it off before you serve them!' says Sid. 'Gordon Bennett! Where did you learn to cook?'

'Watch it, Smart Alec!' says Dad. 'Your mother-in-law has been to evening classes.'

'What in? Vehicle maintenance?' says Sid, unkindly.

'It was no good to me,' sniffs Mum. 'They didn't touch on any of the stuff you can buy down at the supermarket. It was all herbs and that. I'd have to shop at one of those delicate essences – and I'm too old to learn Polish at my age.'

'What is she on about?' says Sid. 'Honestly, sometimes I think the whole lot of you are cracked.'

'Watch it!' says Dad. 'We don't need you to tell us we're cracked.'

'Mum's talking about delicatessens,' I say.

'That's what I said,' says Mum.

'Look, it's all sticking to the celluloid. Disgusting!' Dad waves his kipper about between finger and thumb.

'Now look what you've done! It's covered in fluff.' Mum retrieves Dad's kipper from the cat basket.

'Should keep it warm for you,' says Sid.

'I don't want it now,' says Dad. 'Not after it's been in there. You might as well leave it.'

'No, let Mum have it,' I say. 'You know what they say: Finders kippers.'

I reckon that is a dead funny remark by any standards – witty too. But does it get a laugh? Not on your nelly. The silence reminds me of when I farted at Jerome's christening. Some people have no sense of humour.

I am still cast down when Sid takes me into the front room for a chat. Despite the agrochat that took place earlier he seems in good spirits. 'I've got a real big one,' he says, practically hugging himself.

'Really?' I say. 'That's not what I've heard. Frisky, I grant you, but nothing to start them piling tables against the door at the Over Sixties Club.'

'I'm talking about job opportunities,' says Sid, coldly. 'I know it gets vertigo, but try and drag your mind above crutch level, sometimes.'

'I'm all ears,' I say. Sid looks as if he is going to say something unpleasant and then controls himself.

'Booze,' he says. 'That's what you'll be carrying. Have you heard of Parsimon and Mandrake?'

I rack my brains. 'Is it one of those home-made wines?'

Sid shakes his head exasperatedly. 'No, you berk! They're wine merchants. They're opening a new branch in Basingstoke and you've got to deliver the gargle.'

'It's a bit of a risk, isn't it?' I say. 'I mean, it's an open lorry.'

'I thought you were going to say that because you're such a grumble,' snorts Sid. 'It so happens that they've chosen us because of the particular advantages that our transport bestows.'

'Very nicely put,' I say. 'What advantages?'

'I used a bit of intelligence,' says Sid.

'Oh dear,' I say. 'That means you've got none left.'

'Watch it,' says Sid. 'Just watch it. I read in the paper that these geezers had had a couple of lorryloads of tiddley half inched. So I put two and two together.' Sid looks into my face expectantly and clenches his fists. I surprise him by saying nothing. 'I was able to explain to them that it was because their lorries were so recognisable that they had all these problems. I said that we were specialists in appearing shabby and broken down so that no tealeaf would ever reckon we had anything worth nicking.'

'Brilliant, Sid,' I say. 'Quite brilliant. I suppose you told them how we looked after the Crown Jewels, none of which have ever been nicked?'

'Of course, Timmo. I also informed them of all the work we'd done in conjunction with the Bank of England. A building that has never been knocked off to my knowledge.'

'There's nothing there to knock off,' I say. 'Don't you read the papers?'

'Never mind about that. You put on this nice beige overall I've got you, and tuck your hair in the back of the collar. You never thought about getting a Gatsby haircut, have you? They're very becoming.'

'I didn't like the film, Sid.'

'They go down well with the silent majority, too.' Sid looks at me thoughtfully. 'I don't quite know how to phrase this, Timmo, but I'm a bit worried about your record.'

'You mean, *The Love Theme from Confessions of a Window Cleaner*?'

Sid winces. 'No, you berk. I mean your criminal record. That lead nicking and the spell inside. If that came out it could be very bad for the image of the firm.'

'You were inside, Sid. Bentworth Grange. I remember you telling me.'

'Ah, but that was when I was just a kiddy. Youthful high spirits. There's a smack of the mature criminal about you, Timmo.'

'What are you getting round to, Sid?'

Sid takes a deep breath and tries to square his rounded shoulders. The effort is to much for him. 'What I'm trying to say, Timmo, putting it as nicely as I can, is that if you so much as leave a fingerprint on a bottle of mineral water, I'll break every bone in your bleeding body.'

For a moment I am speechless. How could Sid imagine such a thing before the thought has even entered my mind? 'If that's how you feel, we might as well forget the whole thing,' I say, speaking with simple dignity. 'As for your beige overall you can shove it up your—'

'Timmy, please! You know what I'm trying to say. This is a very important job. It could lead to much bigger things. We can't afford any slip-ups. I'm not blaming you. It's your environment. Look around you. Half the stuff in this room has been nicked. It wouldn't be surprising if you had the same easy-going attitude towards other people's property. Let's face it, stuff goes very easily when your dad's about.'

Sid is referring to Dad's habit of moving the lost property office where he works to our home. Over the years we must have accumulated more stuff than they have.

'You're trying to say that we're a bunch of tealeaves, aren't you?' I tell him.

'I'm not trying to say it, I am saying it!'

Sid is really asking for a punch up the throat. It is lucky for him that he is talking to a devout coward.

'Just a minute, George Washington,' I tell him. 'Before I put you forward for a Duke of Edinburgh's Award, where did that nice beige overall come from?'

Sid turns scarlet. 'I can't remember exactly.'

'Still got the hanger in it, and all,' I say. 'And the price tag. Skidmores. That's the place down the High Street, isn't it? Where they hang all the stuff outside the shop? I bet if I went and asked them if they'd had anything nicked recently they'd give me a very interesting answer.'

'All right, Kojak,' says Sid. 'I'm not saying I'm perfect. I'm just saying watch it, that's all. And mind how you go with that overall. If you mess it up, you'll have to nick the next one yourself.'

When we get round to Parsimon and Mandrake I can see what Sid is worrying about. All that booze is a very tempting sight. Carton after carton of it. Brandy, rum, vodka. All guaranteed to make you irresistible to birds and give you brewer's droop at the same time – not that the ads ever mention the last bit. It is sad when you think about it, isn't it? Booze gives you the desire and takes away your ability to fulfil it. It is like getting a crush on a waste disposal unit.

This is a two lorry job and Sid gets me loaded up first.

'We don't want to travel in convoy,' he says. 'That might arouse suspicion. You go on ahead and I'll follow behind. If you run into any problems, I'll be able to help you out. Don't stop unless you have to. There shouldn't be any problems once you hit the M3. Any questions?'

'Only one,' I say. 'Are we going to get fighter cover?'

Sid says something very unpleasant and I am not sorry to start wending my way towards my appointment with the motorway. The booze is under cover so there is no reason why anybody should suss me out unless they have X-ray eyes.

All goes well till I get to the motorway and then I begin to feel peckish and in need of a pee. It is always the same, when you can't have something – you immediately want it. I keep an eye on the rear mirror for Sid, but there is no sign of him. I think about stopping for a slash beside the motorway but decide against it. Percy is always very bashful about appearing in public and the wind can play some very nasty tricks with your directional equipment. There are few things worse than risking frostbite of the chopper and ending up with a turn-up full of wee and a coach load of school girls taking the piss out of you more effectively than you seem to be capable of doing for yourself.

When I get to a turn-off five miles short of Basingstoke I take the A30 and keep my eyes open for a likely caff. The load can't come to any harm if I sit somewhere where I can keep an eye on it. Within a few miles I come across a likely spot. The Lazy S. There are a stack of lorries parked outside so the nosh must be all right. I tool up to the end of the row and turn off the Yarmouth. I must say that Enid has been no trouble, so far. I give her a friendly pat as I walk round the load to make sure that everything is still lashed down securely. Everything seems to be in order so I step behind a blooming great furniture van and – blimey! I walk straight into an elephant.

As elephants go it is very normal. Large and grey with a hide like weathered cardboard and a few obvious indications that there is a fortune waiting for the man who makes jumbo size toilet tissues a reality rather than a description of the stuff humans use.

What is unusual about it is the bird perched across its neck. She is dressed like a gypsy with big gold earrings, a head scarf and a flouncy dress that rides up provocatively around the place where her legs meet – I forget what it is called, now. She has dark flashing eyes and a pair of well-rounded knockers that jut out proudly, obscuring part of my view of the sky – not that I am so worked up about it that I intend to complain to Patrick Moore.

She and her elephant are at the head of a procession that includes a smaller elephant, a couple of llamas and a chimpanzee led by a sad-faced bloke dressed up as a clown. As they trudge along, it is difficult to decide which looks sadder, the chimp or the bloke. While I am taking in the spectacles, the lead elephant suddenly veers off to the right and sticks its trunk under my tarpaulin. Saucy behaviour, I am certain you will agree.

'Watch it, Dumbo,' I say. 'Keep your hooter to yourself.'

'I'm sorry,' says the bird, giving the beast a sharp tap on the side of the bonce. 'You must be carrying alcohol. Rajah is very partial to a tipple.'

'His senses mislead him,' I say hurriedly. 'This is washing up liquid, every last bottle of it.'

'Oh dear.' The bird shakes her head. 'Poor old thing. He's getting a bit past it.'

'It's sad when they get like that,' I say. 'I'd buy him a pint but I'm a bit pushed for time.'

'That's very kind,' says the bird. 'Are you fond of animals?'

'I like the big ones,' I say. 'I think I get it from my Aunt Edna. She had a soft spot for elephants.'

'What a remarkable woman,' says the bird. 'Is she still with us?'

‘Yes and no,’ I say. ‘Not a hundred percent. You know how it is.’

‘Of course,’ says the bird. ‘Well, I must be on my way.’

‘That’s right,’ I say. ‘Don’t let me hold you up.’

‘If you could, I’d be able to get you a job with the circus,’ says the bird.

We enjoy a little laugh at this pleasantry and take our leave of each other. It has all been very civilised and if I ever have to talk to a woman who is sitting on an elephant again, I hope it will all go as smoothly.

I am pretty certain that the lady did not come from the same country as the elephant because she has ‘Gladys’ embroidered on the back of her dress – the bird that is, not the elephant – and none of those verbal mannerisms which suggest acquaintance with Eastern climes. I would put her down as springing from South Norwood at a pinch – in fact, even without a pinch.

I watch the procession making its way down the road towards Basingstoke and go into the Lazy S wondering whether, when they talk about the lure of the big top, they are referring to Gladys’s knockers. They would certainly keep the rain off you for a couple of hours.

When I get inside the Lazy S, the atmosphere is what Mum would call ‘fraught’. One of the Llamas apparently disgraced itself on top of the juke box. It was playing a Gary Glitter record at the time but nobody is trying to make an issue of it. I just hope it is not a form of criticism that catches on. I was planning on sinking a quick fry up but the llama has managed to change all that. I buy a chocolate bar and throw it away after one bite. Best to get back on the road and finish the job.

When I come out of the caff, the rain is pissing down and I am soaked, even though I sprint to Enid. The windscreen wipers jerk into action and creak from side to side half a dozen times before packing up. Great! I suppose they never needed windscreen wipers in the old days. Mum was always telling me about those summers when the sun never stopped shining and there were no atomic tests. I think about hanging on till the rain stops but the sky looks like a lead sponge and I can't see it drying out in a hurry. Added to that, I am an impetuous little sod. I wind down the window and stick my bonce out just far enough to clock an eyeful of rain and a gander at what is happening ahead. It is not easy but I think I can manage. I ease out the clutch, Enid gives a ladylike squeak and wheezes out of the parking lot. The frog and toad is like a shake and shiver (frog and toad: road; shake and shiver: river. Ed.) and after a few hundred yards I am reckoning myself a prize berk for having started out on this caper. The Queen of Spain is chucking down even faster and I can hardly see anything. At least I am in a nice snug driving cab and not on the back of an elephant. I don't fancy Gladys's job.

No sooner has the thought of the shapely curve carnival flashed across my impressionable mind than I catch sight of a caravan moving even slower than I am. I overtake it and come abreast of another one being towed along in a sea of spray. I am concentrating so hard on getting past it rather than through it that I don't keep my eyes on the road ahead. Suddenly, dead in front of me, is an elephant. I accelerate to get past the caravan, try to cut in front of the car that is towing it in order to avoid jumbo, and go into a four-wheel skid. CRASH! I hit something much harder than an elephant and feel Enid tilt up and over while I crack my head against the driving wheel. The sensation of turning over and over seems to go on for minutes and then I feel myself crumpled up like a piece of paper pushed into the toe of a wet boot. Above my head is an open skylight and through it I can see the grey sky and feel the rain on my face. A head and shoulders appear, looking down at me anxiously.

'Are you all right, mate?' I try stretching a few favourite limbs and nod, managing to bash my head on the dashboard. 'I think so,' I say.

I have a vague recollection of being hauled out of the cab and finding Enid lying on her side against a roundabout but nothing after that until I open my eyes and find myself staring at a pair of legs that end just above crutch level. It gives me a nasty shock, I can tell you. The bird's (she must be a bird because legs like that don't belong to any fellers I know) fun box is pulsating like it has a heart beat and for a few seconds I wonder if I have snuffed it and ended up in some economy style heaven – half a bird is better than nothing, and be thankful for what you've got, you ungrateful little basket!

I then see that I am in a caravan and that the bird is performing some exercise in which she tilts backwards until her forehead is practically resting on the floor behind her. She straightens up and I find myself looking at Gladys.

'Hello,' she says. 'How are you feeling?'

'Fine,' I say, without bothering to check. 'What's happened?'

'You hit the roundabout,' she says, doing the splits. 'I'm afraid it was partly Rajah's fault. He must have thought he was in the ring and sat down on the patch of grass in the middle.'

'What about the – my load?' I say.

Gladys waves a scolding finger at me. 'You're a fibber, aren't you? Trying to make me think that poor old Rajah was losing his grip. You've got enough drink on that lorry to stock a brewery.'

'I was worried about being jacked off – I mean hi-jacked,' I say. Is is all right? I'd better go and—'

'Best not to move for a few minutes.' Gladys presses me back against the bed with surprising firmness. 'Sometimes these things can have delayed effects. There's been a few breakages but nothing too serious.'

'What's that noise?' I say.

'You mean, the sound like an elephant trumpeting?'

'I suppose so,' I say.

'That's Rajah. He's very high-spirited.'

'As long as he's not high on spirits,' I say.

Glady's eyes open wide for a moment before she laughs. 'Oh yes, very good. You do have a sense of humour, don't you?'

'You've got to, these days,' I say. 'Tell me, why are you doing all those exercises?'

Gladys hugs one of her legs to her chest so that it is scraping the ceiling of the caravan. 'It's part of my act,' she says. 'We're only a small circus and we all have to do more than one thing.'

'You have to bend over backwards to help each other,' I say.

'That's right. It doesn't disturb you, does it?'

'I wouldn't say that disturb is the right word,' I say.

'Some people say that it makes them feel uncomfortable.'

'I think it's very artistic,' I say. 'You obviously have a natural bent for it.'

A long time ago I came across – literally, as it so happens – an acrobatic dancer called Sonia and memories of this stimulating encounter are not slow to come flooding back. Could history be on the point of repeating itself?

'What are you thinking?' says the bird.

'Nothing.' I say. In fact, I am wondering if you could

get into her like that. I mean, with one of her legs at the slope arms. It would probably be like trying to put on a french letter while it is still in the packet.

'You must be thinking about something.'

'If you must know, I was thinking how nice it would be if you got into bed with me.'

I hear my voice almost as if it belongs to someone else. I meant what I said but I didn't mean to say it, if you know what I mean. Sometimes there is a bit of a devil inside you that takes over before the 'pleased to meet you' merchant starts clearing his throat.

Gladys drops her foot to floor level and puts her hands on her hips. 'You've recovered quickly, haven't you?' she says. There is no anger in her voice. No surprise. She might be a nurse looking at a thermometer.

'Is your name Gladys?' I ask.

'Yes. How do you know?'

'I saw it on your back. When you were on the elephant.'

Sometimes, I think that being able to communicate with words is actually a bar to making progress with birds. They get in the way. If you were a caveman you would just wack her over the nut with your club and drag her back to your cave. If you were an animal you would run round her three times wagging your tail and then jump on her. She would know what to expect and it would all be very simple. Words add another dimension that complicates everything. It can become like letting the grub grow cold because you are worried about which fork to use.

'Move over, then.'

She whips up her T-shirt and my mince pies enjoy a banquet of naked knocker. She must have been thinking the same as me. Thank goodness she was prepared to do something about it. I bet there are millions of couples who get right to the brink and then funk it. They walk home kicking themselves, knowing that one little word or gesture would have tipped the balance. I can talk about it because I have done it myself. Everybody has, one time or the other. I move across the bed so fast that I bash my bum against the side of the caravan. Somebody has thoughtfully removed my shoes and jeans. I wonder who?

'You've got wonderful breasts,' I say.

I usually find it difficult to flatter birds but in this case it is no problem. You wouldn't see a better pair of bristols in a picture gallery. They are big and shapely with nipples like brown gherkins. Not the puncture patches you find on some of the barrage balloon variety.

'I bet you say that to all the girls,' she says, whipping down her tights with an inviting crackle of nylon.

This is a difficult one to answer because I do say it to all the girls. If not about their knockers then something else. You seldom find a bird who has nothing favourable to comment on even if it is only the tattoo on her left bicep. A kind word does not cost you much and it pays tremendous dividends with the ladies. As I have said many times before, the way to get a reputation for truthfulness amongst women is to tell them that they are beautiful – or that something about them is.

I look at Glady's naked body with a touch of apprehension. It seems normal enough, but so does a pair of nutcrackers until you see them in action. I am also worried about my ability to keep my end up in the coming bout of in and out. I am not referring purely – or impurely – to the lead in the pencil but the pictures I can draw with it. Though no stranger to the manly sport of dongler dousing I do not have a double joint in my body and can only touch my toes after a couple of pints and a goal-charged, blood-warming edition of Grandstand Soccer Preview to fire my athletic imagination. In these circumstances, is it likely that I will be able to keep pace with Jumbo Lady?

Nor is the physical challenge of Gladys all I have to contend with. There is a tremendous noise of honking and hooting close at hand and voices raised in anger. Also the sound of a second elephant doing a Louis Armstrong imitation. Maybe I had better forget about the game of furry quoits and —

'Move over.' Gladys interposes her body between mine and the call of duty. 'It's not very big, is it?'

Her words wound me. 'It gets bigger,' I say, trying to preserve my dignity.

'I'm talking about the bed,' she says.

'I realise that,' I lie, hurriedly. 'I thought perhaps, you could screw a bit on it.'

'You can, darling. You can!' Gladys squirms her body against mine and hooks one of her legs over my thighs.

Something lurches against the side of the caravan but I don't pay too much attention. When the demon lust begins to close his fingers round you, all those promises you made in the boy scouts go clear out of the window. I am certain that whatever problems have arisen at the roundabout are being taken good care of.

'What's this, then?'

Something tells me that Gladys is asking what is known as a rhetorical question. The practised ease with which her fingers latch on to my hampton suggest that this is not the first visit they have paid to the inside of a pair of Y-fronts.

'I don't know,' I say. 'I was going to ask you about it.'

'He's a gentleman whatever he is,' says Gladys. 'He certainly believes in rising for a lady.'

The practised ease with which Gladys's mitts range over my minge throttler would graft backbone into a plate of soft roes. I run my own fingers up the small of her back while my roses browse over her front. I find that women have differing degrees of sensation in the knocker department and it is soon clear that the mammarial caress looms large amongst the things that make life bearable for Gladys.

'Oooh, that's lovely,' she says. 'When you tweak them, it's ooooooh!' So saying, she puts a hammerlock on my hampton that threatens to turn it into one of the longest chipolatas below a line drawn from the crude to the downright filthy.

Fortunately, when I open my mouth to yelp, her nipple drops out and the spell is broken – to say nothing of my knackers.

'I'm sorry,' she says. 'We'd better put him out of harm's way, hadn't we?' So saying, she pulls back the blankets and rises up above me. Before I can threaten to call for help she has bunged her snatch on my love wand and six and a quarter inches of glorious, firm flesh have the daylight denied to them. The lady must have very remarkable internal arrangements because the grip exerted on my action man kit is sufficient to draw a champagne cork. Gladys's minge does not glide up and down the slippery pole of my Mad Mick but pumps it up and down as if using it as a pestle to pound my balls to powder. If this is being put out of harm's way I hate to think what the lady would do if she really had it in for me – as opposed to merely had it in for me.

'Stand by,' she yodels. 'I'm going to give you a hip role.'

'What's that – wheeeeeech!!' I screech. Gladys gives a quick twitch of her educated hips and a ruckle runs up my Marquis of Lorne and rings the bell at the top with enough vibration to rattle my beechams. Talk about muscle control. She has got more grip than Joseph Stalin.

'Give me a bit of notice the next time you do that,' I

gulp. 'Like, about three months – aaaaargh! !'

Regular readers may connect the appearance of an unbroken row of 'a's with the arrival of man's best friend. They would be wrong. What has triggered off my vocal chords is not only the whiplash flexing of elephant lady's thighs but the appearance of one of her charges through the window of the caravan. Not, fortunately, all of him, but merely the trunk, gripping a bottle of gin with the top smashed off. The sight might have been less frightening had the window been open at the time.

No sooner have I responded to this alarming sight than the door of the caravan bursts open and Sid is revealed. The expression on his face leads me to wish that it was his hooter poking through the window while Rajah was before us, winding himself up for a few words.

'What the bloody hell do you think you're doing! !' he says after a couple of moments splutter. Once again, it occurs to me that the answer to this question is well known to the asker. I, of course, am not doing anything, but this information, relayed to Sidney, is hardly likely to change his attitude to the scene now bombarding his eye-balls.

'Hello, Sid,' I say cheerfully.

Gladys is less prepared to extend the hand of welcome 'Get out!' she shouts. 'Push off, you dirty sod!'

I note that her grip on my action man kit does not slacken. If anything, like a cat menaced by someone seeking to remove its prey, she huddles over me protectively.

'Do you know what's going on out there?' sobs Sid. 'There's hardly anything left of your load. There's a traffic jam stretching back two miles in all directions and there isn't one vehicle not heavier by the weight of a bottle of scotch.'

'What about the police?' I say. 'Surely the police have arrived?'

Sid delivers what I believe is known as a hollow laugh. 'Oh yes,' he says. 'They've arrived all right. We've got them here from four counties. What I want to know is, how you can lie there getting your end away while our livelihood is disappearing up the spout? And you, missus. You might stop while I'm talking to him!'

But Gladys is not a lady easily prepared to foresake her pleasures. Ignoring Sidney, she continues to throttle percy with her third hand whilst my open cakehole strives to deliver a few words of comfort to my clearly harassed brother-in-law.

'Hold on a minute,' I say. 'I'm just com-com-com-com-coming!!!'

For a moment, I think I am going to develop a permanent kink in my snatch pounder as the lady's complicated internal workings give a formidable imitation of an electric mixer. Perhaps disturbed by the noises I am making, the elephant drops the bottle of gin on the end of the bed and rips open the wall of the caravan as if it is a piece of newspaper. Sid steps back hurriedly and falls down the steps. It is still pouring with rain as I realise when a small fountain of water fills the spot where Sid was standing.

'He's drunk!' shouts Gladys.

'I don't think so,' I say. Then, I realise that she is probably talking about the elephant. The creature is snuffling round my foot with its trunk. It occurs to me that it might well have a protective instinct towards its mistress – if not something even more unwholesome, and this thought is substantiated as it tries to throw me out of bed. Gladys is strong in the pelvic area but she cannot compete with an elephant and I hit the floor like a moggy that has been turfed out of an armchair. I am now aware that there are a number of bedraggled faces watching what is happening inside the caravan with something not far short of extreme interest. Most of them are clutching bottles of spirits and the sight of my erstwhile cargo disappearing down alien throats makes me begin to heed Sid's words – the fact that I have just shot my own load makes it easier to face up to reality as well.

'Get out of there!' shouts Sid, struggling up the steps and trying to grab my arm.

'Hang on a minute,' I tell him. 'I've got my pants on the wrong way round.'

'That doesn't matter. You're not going to need the slit when I've finished with you!'

'There's quite a simple explanation for all this,' I say as Sid bundles me out into the rain. 'I'll think of it if you give me a few moments.'

'Look at that!' says Sid.

I follow his shaking finger and, I must confess, it is a most remarkable sight. The caravan, amongst others, is parked on the verge near the roundabout and every approach road as far as the eye can see is jammed with traffic.

'You'd have thought that they would have moved the lorry by now,' I say.

'They're not doing badly,' says Sid, grimly.

I look again and see what he means. Most of the blokes round Enid are staggering away with as much booze as they can carry. It is like a swarm of ants round a blob of jam. One of the elephants is lying in the middle of the roundabout with its feet in the air and the chimpanzee is sitting on top of the cab passing down bottles of brandy to a bloke with a peaked cap who looks like a chief inspector.

'That's enough of that, constable,' he is saying as I approach. 'Let's have a few more of those vintage port.'

The copper's face is not unknown to me. 'Inspector McGoolygrab?'

The bule thrusts a crate of scotch into my hands. 'Put that in the boot, laddy.'

'I'm the driver of this vehicle,' I say. 'May I ask why you are removing its load?'

'Drink this,' says the dreaded McG, practically shoving a bottle into my cakehole. 'What does that taste like?'

'Brandy,' I say.

'Are you sure? Try again.' He tilts the fat end of the bottle skywards so that the booze spills down the front of my shirt.

'Positive,' I splutter.

'Right, constable. Take this man away and breathalyse him. By the throbbing tip of my wangy truncheon I'll wager that the bag will turn so green we won't have to add dye.'

The chimpanzee drops from the cab and starts to lead me away past two constables who are dancing with each other on the verge – quite what they are on the verge of I don't like to think for fear of upsetting my more sensitive readers.

'You swine!' I shout. 'This is a frame-up.'

McGoolygrab does not answer. He is too busy wrenching the top off a tin of cashew nuts.

'Another fine mess you've got us in to!' I turn to find Sid at my side. That is all you need at a moment like this, a chimpanzee on one side and Sid on the other.

'What are we going to do?' I ask.

Sid looks round. Gladys is trying to remonstrate with one of the elephants that has just dropped the police car and started to throw bottles through the windows of the caravans and the two llamas are demonstrating that their feelings for each other are more than purely platonic. The rain is sluicing down and a party of schoolgirls are vacating their coach and clambering eagerly into the back of a five-ton lorry full of soldiers. The soldiers look eager too.

Sid takes a deep breath. 'Slip your friend a banana and let's get out of here.'

CHAPTER FIVE

In which Timmy and Sid come unstuck in a transport cafe and Timmy cements a union with a nurse travelling to Manchester.

What makes the whole thing worse is that Sid's lorry has been nicked. Yes, terrible, isn't it? We walk half a mile down the queue of traffic and then another half mile because Sid thinks that he must have mistaken the layby. With every step of the second half mile the stream of abuse that is pouring from his lips begins to falter to a trickle and then completely dry up as the horrible truth comes home to him.

Thank God that the booze is insured, otherwise we might really be in the cart. When we eventually recover Enid there are only half a dozen bottles of Tizer left on board. Sid's vehicle is found on the outskirts of Wolverhampton. All the booze has gone and somebody has left a 'naughty Fido' on the driver's seat. Some people have no consideration, have they? Needless to say we do not get any further commissions from Parsimon and Mandrake and, for a few weeks, things are very dicey generally. Most of our roadwork is done driving down to the Labour to collect our benefit. It is more like being self-unemployed than self-employed. Then slowly things begin to pick up. We do a bit of humping for a local scrap merchant and Sid has a mate who runs a factory that makes cork mats. We take a few loads of his stuff up to Manchester and pick up tropical plants that we unload at Birmingham. Then it is garden tools back to London. It is not exactly 'The Wages of Fear' but we make a living.

After a few weeks I begin to feel a bit of an old hand. I

nod at blokes when I go into caffs and there is a geezer I help when his load comes unstuck who actually flashes his lights at me before I flash him. I even catch a glimpse of Shirley. She is bending herself double to get into an E-type Jag that has left a couple of inches of tyre over three hundred feet of road in an effort to stop beside her. One long leg flickers wickedly from her coat like a snake's tongue and then is withdrawn from view. The door slams and the crouching greyhound springs forward and roars past me in a blurr of red. I think about that leg and the red blurr is replaced by a green blurr: jealousy. I shove my foot down on the accelerator and Enid reacts as if I have just kicked her in the stomach and signals that another two miles per hour and a tortured whine is all that she is capable of. I don't think she has liked me very much since the roundabout incident. The Jag is disappearing over the brow of the road. I imagine Shirley's knees pressed up against the dashboard and her coat dropping open to reveal the long sweep of her thighs . . . Enid's scream becomes lughole-piercing and I ease my foot off the accelerator. One day . . . One fine day, I will catch up with lovely Shirl.

One of the hazards of the game is the grub they serve at some of the caffs. You would think that after Mum's cooking I would be able to take anything but the reverse is true. I am very sensitive about what my Teds bite into and some of the nosh they serve up would incite a mass break out at a pig farm. When I ask for a bowl of soup, I want to drink it, not use it to stick Formica.

There is one place in particular where even the bluebottles won't go for fear of getting food poisoning. I usually drive straight past but one day, when I am with Sid, he makes a particular point of asking me to pull over.

'You don't want to stop there,' I tell him. 'It's diabolical.'

'I know it is,' says Sid, not without relish. 'I nearly had a punch-up there and the bloke threatened to set his Alsatian on me.'

'So why do you want to go back?'

Sid pats the pocket of his flying jacket. 'You'll see.'

When we get through the door, the smell of fat nearly makes the contents of my Derby Kell play ring-a-ring-a-roses on the two thirty Rory (two thirty: dirty; Rory O'More: floor. Ed). or to put it more simply, I nearly toss a technicolor pancake.

'Order a cup of tea and sit down,' says Sid. This is one of the few places I know where they serve chips with every cup of tea – around the rim of the cup. The tea is not only the colour of mahogany – it tastes like it.

'I'll have a coke,' I say. 'They can't mess about with that.'

As it turns out, I am not so sure. The old bag behind the counter pours it into a cloudy glass the colour of the one Dad keeps his dentures in. In fact, I am so worried that I have a poke about at the bottom with a teaspoon. I need not have alarmed myself, there is only a piece of chewing-gum.

'What did you want to come here for?' I ask. 'Do they have a tea dance or something?'

'Belt up,' says Sid. 'I'm waiting for the right bloke to come along.'

'Blimey!' I say. 'I must say, you've kept it a wonderful secret. All these years and you were a ginger. How does Rosie feel about it?'

'Swallow your lips, will you?' Sid is not looking at me but studying the geezers who are coming in to the caff. 'He'll do.' The bloke Sid has singled out looks like a gorilla in a blue overall. If his barnet started growing half an inch lower, his hair line would be below his mince pies.

'You go for the brutal type, don't you?' I say.

Sid waves his hand in my face. 'Belt up, Cinderella. I want to hear what his number is.'

In this place, when you order your nosh, you get given a number. You sit down and when the cook has finished squirting greasy germs over it, your number is called and you put on a pair of thick gloves and go and collect it. I think the expression 'your number's up', meaning that you are about to snuff it, originated in this place.

'One hundred and thirty-two,' I say. 'Blimey, no wonder the stomach powder dispenser is empty.'

'Sit tight,' says Sid. 'When that bloke's got his grub I want you to go and distract his attention for a moment. Ask him for a light or something like that.'

'I'll tell him that you fancy him,' I say. 'That should arouse his interest.'

'Tell him how you got your broken nose,' says Sid, menacingly.

'What is all this about?' I ask.

Sid looks round and produces something from his breast pocket. 'Recognise it?' he asks.

'It's a fried egg!' I say.

'Not so loud, you berk! It's made of rubber. It just looks like a fried egg. While you're distracting the bloke's attention I'll do a switch and he'll tuck into the imitation job.' Sid allows himself a malicious smile. 'I reckon he'll kill the bloke who runs this place after the first mouthful.'

I shake my head in admiration. 'That's a conception of truly diabolical cunning,' I say. 'Expensive, too. How much did that egg cost?'

'I confiscated it from Jason,' says Sid. 'Cheeky little

Charley 'Arstard tried it on me at breakfast. Hang on! Here we go.'

'One-three-two' echoes over the loudspeaker system and the Gorilla shambles to his feet. He is an ugly looking cove, there is no doubt about it. I would not like him to find me with my all forlorn being the cause of a chink of light showing between his old lady's walkabouts. The very thought of it casts a cold shadow along the length of my giggle stick. The man collects a plate of petrified morsels from the engine driver's assistant behind the counter and returns to his seat via the cash desk. It may be my imagination but I think I see the eyes of the old slag who takes the money move. It must be getting near the time when she changes her skin.

'All right, Robert Redford,' says Sid. 'Get out there and do your stuff.' He is practically humming the theme music from *The Sting*. He is very impressionable is Sid.

I stand up, replace the watered-down bottle of HP sauce I have knocked down and direct my animal grace towards the Gorilla's table. A number of ruses pass through my computer mind but in the end I decide to settle for Sid's suggestion. Should anything go wrong, he will only have himself to blame. Checking that Clapham's answer to Paul Newman is on the right course I clear my throat and close with the Gorilla.

'Excuse me, mate. Have you got a light?'

The giant fist returns the fork to the side of the yellowing plate and dives into the pocket of the donkey jacket. It is at this point that I realise that I don't have a cigarette. The Gorilla produces a box of Swan Vestas and starts to go through the motions of striking one of them. A feeling not totally unakin to panic descends upon me. The match flares into flame and the Gorilla looks at me expectantly.

'Have you got a cigarette as well?' I say, trying to inject

a pleasing lilt into my voice. Whatever Sid may think of the way I have done it, there is no doubt at all that I have succeeded in distracting the Gorilla's attention.

'Have I what?!!' The vast hulk of the bloke towers above me. I am vaguely aware of Sid doing his stuff but it is not my first area of consideration.

'I'm sorry. I – er—' I try to back away but a giant mit descends on my jacket.

'Are you trying to take the piss?' I splutter convincingly.

'You buy your own bleeding fags!!' The Gorilla signals the end of our conversation by thrusting me back half a dozen paces. Everybody in the caff is looking at us and I feel a right berk. With my cheeks burning, I scuttle back to Sid.

'You didn't have to overdo it,' he says contemptuously. 'I thought you were trying to start a punch-up.'

'Did you get the egg?' I say.

Sid nods at the table in front of me. 'What does that look like?'

'It looks like the rubber one covered in blue fluff,' I say.

'I had to slip it in my pocket,' says Sid. 'You can have it if you like.' I don't think he is joking either. 'Hang on, here he goes.'

The Gorilla gives me a farewell scowl and empties a bottle of watered-down tomato ketchup over his plateful. Sid rubs his hands together and leans forward in anticipation. The Gorilla picks up his irons and I suck in my breath. In a couple of seconds, he will be going berserk. It may be that our little brush will help to make him even angrier. I wink at Sid and my lips part in an anticipatory smile. It is like when one of the blokes at school put tin tacks on the teacher's chair and we all waited for him to sit down.

'Now!' Sid bites his tongue and the Gorilla shovels home the first mouthful. No reaction. This time! Still no reaction. Maybe he is saving the egg until last or it has got lost under all the ketchup. The Gorilla takes another mouthful and spreads out a crumpled copy of *The Sun.*

Sid looks at me and shakes his head. 'What's up with him?' I shrug my shoulders and Sid rises to his feet like a man in a dream. The Gorilla is staring at a full page photo of Nadine Jardine who likes horse riding, dancing and baring her knockers to readers of *The Sun*. I know because I looked at a copy earlier. Sid walks past the Gorilla's table and beckons to me as he heads for the Gents. I follow him, but not past the Gorilla's table.

'What happened, Sid?' I say.

'He ate it,' says Sid.

It all goes to show why we have such diabolical nosh in this country. People will eat anything. Even a rubber egg covered in tomato ketchup.

'I'm amazed the knife was sharp enough to cut through it,' muses Sid. 'He must have put it in all at once.'

Putting it in all at once makes me think automatically of some of the birds of passage who hang around the transport caffs. Most of them are not very lovely but they are yours for the price of a bacon sandwich and a night's kip in your cab. They are travelling ladies and they must see more of this country than the British Travel Association ever dreamed of. They would be offended if you called them nails. With them it's more a question of barter: 'a ride for a ride' is how the professionals describe it. Like I say, most of them would stand out at the vicar's tea party like a donkey's erection but there are exceptions. They don't all use their faces as full colour advertisements for the services they offer. Shirl is a good example. I ask some of the old boilers I give a lift to about her and the ones that know her reckon that she is too stuck up for her own good. 'She doosn't give a booger for anywoon,' says one of them. 'She's disappointed a loot of poiple.'

I take this to mean that she does not always deliver the goods in the manner laid down by the conventions of the road. This is not something that can be said about most of my travelling companions. Some of them are very insistent on making their contribution for services rendered. I don't think that there is any doubt that they fancy the life. I find that the best thing to do when faced with an offer I can easily refuse is to say that I am recovering from a bout of The Coachman (Coachman on the box: pox. Ed.). This way you don't give offence.

One bird who gives me a big surprise is a little nurse I pick up in North London. She is wearing her uniform and carrying an overnight bag and she looks a dead ringer for Florence Nightingale. You would not reckon that you could get a thermometer up her 'how's your father?' let alone anything else.

'Where are you going to?' she says, looking up at me like Little Red Riding Hood must have looked at the wolf.

'How does Manchester grab you?' I say.

'Marvellous,' she says. 'It must be my lucky day.'

She hands up her hold-all and scrambles into the cab like a kid being shown the inside of an aeroplane's cockpit.

'It's nice,' she says. 'Cosy. Would you like a sweetie?' She produces a brown paper bag and shoves it in front of my face.

'Ta,' I say. 'What are they?'

'Bulls eyes. They're a bit sticky. Shall I pop one in for you?'

'Ta.' I open my cake hole and she gives me a lovely

smile as she slots the goody between my Teds. She has dark curly hair, big brown eyes and a dust of freckles round her button nose. She is so wholesome she makes an Ovaltine Girl seem like Lucretia Borgia.

'Do you want to do it now or later?' she says.

For a moment, I think I must have misheard her. 'I'm sorry,' I say. 'I don't get you.'

'Sex,' she says, without blinking. 'Here or at the other end? There's a good place just off this layby we're coming to.'

You can imagine my feelings. Deep and profound shock coupled with a keen sense of moral outrage and a strong dose of 'can't wait to get at it!'

'Where?!' I say, nearly unscrewing the steering wheel as I wrench it over.

'Through the trees at the end,' she says, hauling herself up into the vertical. 'I hope you don't think I'm fussy but I travelled with this feller who had me on the side of the A6 in broad daylight. Anybody could have seen.'

'You go up north a lot, do you?' I ask, steering Enid between a couple of silver birches.

'When I get a long leave,' she says. 'My parents live in Salford. The train fares are terrible, aren't they? I'd never go if I had to save up the fare.'

'Uum,' I say. I still haven't quite cottoned on to the idea of this bird offering herself to me as the price of the trip north. 'Is this how you normally do it?'

'That's right,' she says. 'I don't mind returning a favour. Do you want to stay inside? It's probably better, isn't it? You never know who's about, these days.' She props her legs against the front of the cab, raises her bum, and slips off a pair of navy blue panties. 'Put these in your pocket, will you? I don't want to lose them. And my sweeties.'

I do as I am told, hardly able to believe my luck. 'This happens every time, does it?'

The bird stretches out her hand for my zip. 'You should know. Oh, sorry. My fingers are sticky from those sweets.'

'I'm not complaining,' I say.

'Have you got anything to wipe them on?'

I tug down my zipper. It is like pulling the string on a self inflating dinghy. 'Use that,' I say.

CHAPTER SIX

In which Timmy meets Henrietta, a lady of refinement who has been assaulted in a layby, and strange goings on ensue.

Hannah, that is the bird's name. Nurse Hannah Dobson. We have another bit before I drop her and it is even better than the first time. When I think about it, it usually is. You're more relaxed, I suppose. More relaxed, but still finding each other new and exciting. I tell her that I'll keep my eye open for her but I never see her again. Sad, isn't it? I think about her every time I pass that layby – well, nearly every time. As the weeks go past, more and more laybys start to hold memories for me. It is amazing some of the things you see.

Once darkness falls half the population seems to be at it in the back of a car. There are laybys I can think of where the peeping toms are queuing up like buskers outside a West End cinema. Of course, most of these geezers wearing out their springs are up to no good. Stands to reason, doesn't it? If you can afford a Jag you can afford a pad to take your lady friends to. You would not work out on the back seat unless you were kinky for the kiss of imitation leather against your bare bum. It's got to be that the old woman is back home watching 'World in Agony' and hoping that the lamb cutlet in the oven bakes so dry it chokes you. It doesn't have to be the old woman either. I see a number of nifty looking birds in sports cars who are tongue angling with young blokes who don't look as if they could scrape together the wherewithal to buy a plastic valve cap. Their talents function below dashboard level. The birds usually look a bit desperate – like they feel middle age breathing down their necks and know that Edgar is going to start wondering why they have to visit their sister so often.

I mention this as a background to Henrietta. I meet her in a layby. Well, it is not so much a layby as one of those windy bits of road that have been by-passed. They are favourite for back seat bingo. Walk down them and there is hardly a window that does not have a curtain of steam over it.

It is about eleven o'clock at night and I am looking for a place to get my head down for a few minutes – I refer to a kip, not a muff job, I am travelling alone. I pull off at this stretch of road but it is choked with private cars, huddled together like woodlice. I feel choked, too. Both because I am dead knackered and because I resent the thought of somebody else getting their end away while I have to sweat my guts out – there is nothing big hearted about me. I have just got back to the main road without finding a parking space and am silently hoping that the rubber in any french letters being used has perished when my headlights pick out this bird rushing towards me. For a moment, I think she is going to chuck herself under the wheels. Then she stumbles round to my side of the cab and bangs on the door.

'Help, help!' she hollers. 'I've been attacked. Take me to the police!' She looks over her shoulder desperately. 'He's coming after me!'

At least he had some consideration, I think to myself. Now, I hope I don't have to convince anybody that I am lion-hearted in the extreme. The courage of the Leas is a legend. We don't know the meaning of the word fear – amongst many other words. However, our raw adventurous spirit is leavened by a strong dose of common sense – often confused with cowardice by those who don't know us. Although my natural impulse is to leap down into the darkness and sort out the grumble bandit I control myself. There are some very funny people about and fruity nut-cases can turn nasty in the extreme. Maybe better to do as the lady says and let the moody blues sort it out. I mean, that's what they get paid for, isn't it? It's not all raiding dirty book shops and deciding whether to bring an action rather than take a slice of it.

'Hop in,' I say. 'Round the other side.'

She is definitely a harassed lady as I see when she scrambles in beside me. Her blouse is open down to her waist and her bra is all cock-eyed like somebody has had a go at it. Her lipstick is smeared, her eye make-up is running and there is a blotchy flush spreading downwards from her neck. I must say, I find it quite a turn on. I take a gander at the lower half of her body and she immediately smoothes her long woollen skirt over her leather boots like she is protecting herself. She has straight blonde hair cut close to her nut and nervous, slightly zany, blue eyes. I look out into the darkness but I can't see anything.

'Is he coming?'

'I don't think so.'

The bird shivers. 'Please get me away from here.'

I ease forward to the edge of the road. 'Which way? You do want to go to the police?'

'Oh yes. Turn left and keep straight on.' I do as she says and take another look at her out of the corner of my eye. There are no indications that she has been badly roughed up. 'What happened?'

'Have you got a cigarette?'

'I don't use them.'

'Blast!' The bird is really on edge. She sits there, biting her fingernails like a kid watching a horror movie.

A car's headlights appear in the rear view mirror and

she looks up at them nervously. The car overtakes and moves ahead fast. 'We were going home after the drama club. He said he wanted to talk to me.'

'I see.' I don't see, really, but you can't go on asking questions. 'You're all right, are you?'

The bird does not seem to hear me.' He exposed himself to me,' she says.

'Must have been very disturbing for you,' I say.

'I'd never done anything like it before.'

I am not quite certain what she means by this. The way she puts it, it sounds as if she had something to do with what happened. Something she feels ashamed or embarrassed about.

'I keep straight on, do I?' I ask.

The bird bites her lips. 'No, stop.'

'Stop?' I take my foot off the accelerator.

'Maybe it isn't a very good idea. They'd ask a lot of questions, wouldn't they? It would be very embarrassing.'

'It's up to you,' I say. 'I mean, I don't really know what happened. You weren't—? He didn't – er rape you?'

'I wouldn't let him,' says the bird. 'He was saying the most terrible things. Things he wanted to do to me.' She brings her hand to her throat. 'I should never have given him a lift.'

'It was your car, was it?' I say.

The bird looks at me sharply. 'Do you think that makes a difference? Do you think the police will believe that I – I was a party to what happened?'

'You drove to the layby, did you?'

'Yes, but we didn't go there to make love – at least, I didn't. I thought we were going to discuss the play.'

'Yes,' I say.

'You don't believe me, do you?'

'It doesn't matter what I think,' I say. 'You know how

difficult it is to get a charge like this to stick. Then there's your husband. You are married, are you?' The bird nods. 'How's he going to feel about it?'

The bird doesn't say anything for a couple of minutes. 'You're saying that I should forget it?'

'I think maybe that's what you're saying yourself. Wait till tomorrow, anyway.' There is another silence. 'Do you want me to take you back to your car?'

'If you don't mind.' She gives me a nervous smile. 'I'm sorry to cause you all this trouble. You must think I'm a very foolish woman.'

'Oh no,' I say. 'I'm certain it was very nasty for you.' I pull into a garage forecourt and start to turn round.

'I suppose I did act rather stupidly. I think sometimes that I must be very innocent.'

'It makes a change,' I say. The road is clear so I pull out and we start chugging back the way we have come.

'I think it must have been the roles we were playing. It was a romantic comedy, you see. We got on very well. I just wasn't prepared for what happened. It was so – so blatant.'

'I expect he got a bit carried away. I mean, you're not—' I break off and concentrate on my driving.

'What were you going to say?'

'You'd probably think I was like him if I said it. I was going to say that you were very attractive.'

'Thank you.' I can feel the bird weighing me up. 'I don't think it would have been so bad if it had been you, I mean, I don't know you. I haven't formed an impression of you. You could be anything. With John, I'd cast him in a role and he suddenly behaved completely differently to what I expected. That's what startled me. Do you understand what I mean?'

'Sort of,' I say.

'I don't think you do. Not that I blame you. I don't think I understand it myself. I suppose, in a way, I did want an adventure. That's what it boils down to. But I was frightened – a little ashamed of myself.'

'Here we are,' I say. 'Where's the car?'

'Down the end. Just near where you picked me up.' The bird grabs my arm. 'Do you think he's still there?'

'Could be,' I say. 'He hasn't got any other way of getting home has he?'

'Will you go and look?'

I was afraid the judy would say that. The bloke is probably sitting there waiting to bend an iron bar over my nut. 'Is he likely to turn nasty?'

'I don't know. He's usually very quiet. That was one of the things that so surprised me about the way he behaved.'

'Of course, he might have taken the car and pushed off,' I say, looking on the bright side.

'I've got the key.' My spirits drop again. Lady Smart Arse has to think of everything, doesn't she? 'It's over there, the MG.'

I take a deep sigh and my life in my hands. 'You hang on here. I'll have a look round.'

'Thank you,' she says. 'It's most awfully kind of you. I am sorry to be such a nuisance.' She has a very 'refained' voice like one of those birds who buttonholes you on flag days. I bet they love her round at the drama club.

I climb out of the cab and turn up the collar of my jacket. I feel like a gypsy's kiss but it is a pleasure I will have to postpone. I can't see anybody through the window of the MG but I approach it with caution. My torch has packed up and when the moon goes behind the clouds it is darker than Mum's toast. I press my nose up against the window and take a shufti inside. Not a sausage. Thank God for that. The frustrated hampton parker must have pushed off. Either that or he is lurking in the bushes. The thought makes me whip round sharpish. There is no one there but I suppose I must force myself to take a butchers. Blooming neurotic woman! Why didn't she let the bloke get on with it? That way we would all have been better off. I take a quick look in the bushes – they smell like an elephant's graveyard during an undertakers' strike – and head back to the lorry.

I am just passing a small saloon when the door bursts open, nearly knocking me over. In my present highly nervous condition it is enough to make me leap ten feet in the air. When I land, an aggressive looking geezer is waiting for me.

'How would you like a bashed in hooter?' he says.

'Why? Are you trying to give yours away?' I ask him.

The bloke does not seem to find this remark funny. 'Peeping Tom!' he hisses. 'I've a good mind to duff you up!'

'Don't be stupid,' I say. 'You couldn't punch a hole in a rice pudding. I'd rather watch a Party Political Broadcast than you trying to get your end away. I hate to see people suffering.' As can be imagined from my comments, the bloke is much smaller than me. Small but beautifully narked as you might put it.

'I'll report you to the police,' he says.

'Don't be pathetic,' I say. 'Tell me, have you seen a bloke wandering about here?'

'Only you,' he says. 'Lost your boyfriend, have you?'

Further unpleasantness follows, but by the time Shorty has returned to his beloved and I am making tracks for Enid, it is clear that 'Mr Wham! Bam! Thank you Ma'am!' is no longer in the neighbourhood.

'It's OK, there's no one about,' I say, sticking my head inside the cab.

'Thank you so much.' Madam has obviously spent the time I was away tarting herself up. She looks very nice. You would never know that she had been fumbled.

'You'll be all right now, will you?'

'I'd be grateful if you'd stay till I've driven off. I'm sorry, but—'

'OK, OK. Don't apologise.' I help her down and trudge back to the MG. She gets in and winds down the window.

'Thank you so much. I'm sorry I—'

'Don't mention it.' I step back and wait patiently.

The bird feels in the pocket of her jacket. Then in the other pocket. 'Oh dear.'

'You've lost the key, have you?' For some reason, it does not come as a big surprise to me. I don't think I am ever going to see the back of this one.

'I could have sworn that I put it in my pocket.'

'Maybe it fell out in my cab. Hang on a minute.' Back to Enid. There is no sign of an ignition key.

'Yoo hoo!' The bird is waving something at me.

Back to the MG. 'You found it did you?'

'On the floor. I'm sorry, you must think I'm quite mad.'

'It's just not your evening.'

'Well, I'm off now. Thanks again.'

'Don't mention it.'

She leans forward to turn on the ignition and I notice that some of the buttons on her blouse have popped open again. Funny, that. I distinctly remember her doing them up on the way to the Fuzz. She has nice knockers, there is no doubt about it. She struggles with the key and wriggles the driving wheel. Nothing happens.

'Oh dear.'

'What's the matter?'

'I can't turn the ignition. It's got one of those anti-thief devices attached to the steering and it's a bit stiff sometimes.'

'Aren't we all,' I say. 'Listen, you don't think your mate's done something to it, do you?'

'Oh dear,' she says. 'What am I—'

'If you get out a minute, I'll have a look at it.'

'That is kind of you. I'm so—'

'That's all right.' If she says she's sorry again, I'll nut her.

She slides an elegant pair of gams out of the motor and I detect the arousing note of the silk lining of her skirt rubbing against her thighs. I squeeze my way into the car and am slightly surprised to find her climbing in beside me.

'It's cold,' she says.

I am not really concentrating but I can't help noticing her staring at me very strangely. Her right hand goes down to the gear stick and at first I imagine that she is checking that it is in neutral. It is one of those short, stubby jobs – the gear stick, I mean. She runs her fingers up and down the shaft and then starts massaging the knob at the top. I don't know what the sight would do for the Archbishop of Canterbury but it sends shivers through my action man kit, I don't mind telling you. I put it down to the fact that she has been through a harrowing experience and joggle the steering wheel. Immediately, there is a 'click' and I can turn the key in the ignition. The engine roars into life and I rev my foot up and down on the accelerator.

At that moment the bird leans against me and drops her head on my chest. For a moment I think that she has fainted. Her hand stretches out to the dashboard and she switches off the ignition.

'Fuck me!'

I don't think I have ever been so surprised at anything

anybody has said since the vicar spoke out against Jason having a crafty Jimmy Riddle behind the font at nephew Jerome's christening.

'What—?' I say.

I don't get the chance to say more than that because the bird launches herself onto my cakehole like it is the last bus home. Not only that. She yanks up her skirt and guides my hand to her snatch – in fact, she doesn't so much guide it as chuck it. What is so amazing is that she doesn't have any knicks on. And the language she is using. Her opening remark was the script for *Listen with Mother* compared to what is pouring out now.

Well, of course, there is only one thing to do, isn't there? Tell her to pull herself together or you will have to slap her over the wrist with a bag of heavily powdered jelly babies. The trouble is that it doesn't work out like that in practice, does it? The beast between the thighs takes over. Before you can say 'Roger Carpenter with knobs on' we are half out of the car and half in it, the heels of her boots are tapping like castanets in the small of my back, and I am totally immersed in what I am doing. The noise must be enough to waken a cabinet minister but I don't think about that. You never do, do you? There is also a flash of light from the bushes which I put down to some peeping tom's plastic mac going up in flames.

It must be a bag of coke to remember because when I am leaning against a tree, trying to get my breath back, I notice that we have shunted the car three feet sideways. It is a muddy evening but that is still not bad, is it?

Once I have tommed (Tom Thumb: come. Ed.) I begin to wonder about how the lady is going to react to our spot of in and out. It occurs to me that she might suddenly start screaming 'rape!' or show other signs of over-excitement. There is certainly something a tiny bit odd about her. Fortunately, I don't have to worry. She has hardly checked her mug in the driving mirror than she is starting up the engine.

'It seems to be all right now,' she says in her best "thank you James' voice." 'I'm most grateful for your help.'

With these gracious words she switches on her lights and accelerates out of my life, spraying mud all over my jeans. If I did not have the damp knees and the feeling of personal loss around the Y-front area I might be excused for imagining that I had dreamt the whole thing.

Being a person who is deeply interested in the workings of the human mind, especially as they relate to birds and their attitude towards a bit of the other, I think long and earnestly about the motivation for the MG lady's precipitous assault on my person. Eventually I reach the following conclusion. The bird was a stranger to extra-marital relationships but had decided that it was about time that she had a dabble. She had this bloke lined up but was ashamed of how she felt and the things she would like to have done to her. Maybe, the bloke was a friend of her old man and that made it all a bit close for comfort. Anyway, they get to the layby and start having a go at each other. The bird gets worked up, but at the same time she gets frightened – or, even better, she comes on so strong that the bloke gets frightened. Either way, she suddenly finds herself in a situation when everything has stopped and she wishes that it hadn't. Then I come along.

It makes sense, doesn't it? At least, it does until I am sitting in a caff a few weeks later. Near me is this big spotty herbert who is stirring the bottom out of his cup of tea and rabbiting on to his bored mate.

'. . . on the way back from evening classes,' I hear him saying. 'Said she wanted to go to the police about it. She was really worked up.'

'What did they do about it? Give her one, too?'

'Naa! Do me a favour. I'm serious, aren't I?' The bloke drops his voice and leans forward towards his mate. I lean forward too. 'We never got there. She suddenly changes her mind and says she's worried about her old man and how he's got a weak heart.'

'That's because he's been giving her one, and all.'

'Listen! Do you want to hear what happens or not? It's all the same to me.'

'Go on. I won't believe it anyway.'

'We get back to the layby and she suddenly grabs hold of my balls. "I've got to have you! I've got to have you!" She keeps saying it!'

The listener catches my eye and winks. 'I know. It was bleeding Rita Hayworth, wasn't it? I had her last week.'

'Oh, piss off!' says the bloke. 'I don't care what you think. It was bleeding fantastic. She was like an animal. She couldn't get enough of it.'

'No bird can get enough of it from you, that's your problem,' says the second bloke standing up. 'Do you fancy another cuppa?' He picks up his mate's cup and walks past my table. 'Did you ever hear such a load of rubbish?' he says, nodding over his shoulder. 'Poor sod lives in a dream world.'

'That's right,' I say.

CHAPTER SEVEN

In which Timmy and Sid are asked to remove nearly everything by an animated lady who wants her furniture taken to Peterborough.

It is six weeks after we have been 'in operation' as he chooses to call it that Sid gets a good idea. I am so amazed that I don't know what to do. However much I think about it, it still seems like a good idea. It is very disturbing. Eerie almost.

'I don't know why I didn't think of it before,' says Mastermind breezily. 'It's an obvious opportunity to extend the facilities that exist at our fingertips' – he is inclined to express himself like that sometimes, poor berk. 'The Noggett Home Removal Service will fit neatly into the logistical infrastructure of the parent company.'

'Aren't you going to need a furniture van?' I ask.

'In a word – yes,' says Sid. 'I have already acted in the matter.'

'You sound more like you've acted in *Downstairs Upstairs*,' I tell him. 'Try and talk natural for gawd's sake.'

Sid chooses to ignore my comment. 'Furthermore, I have arranged our first commission. Peterborough.'

'Where are we moving it to?' I ask.

Sid smiles weakly. 'You do enjoy your little joke, don't you? We're moving a family to Peterborough. I think if we can fit a few of these removal jobs in amongst our normal activities we'll be on our way to making a few bob.'

'It's going to be hard work,' I say.

'What does that matter?' says Sid. 'Think of the satisfaction you'll be getting. You're your own boss.'

'No, I'm not. You're my own boss.'

Sid's face clouds over. 'I don't like to hear you talk like that, Timmo,' he says. 'I don't think of the relationship between us as being that of boss and employee. We're partners in one of life's great adventures. It's a marriage of opportunities. We're both working for us.'

'Does that mean I'm going to get some money soon?' I ask.

'You have to spoil everything, don't you?' says Sid. 'Mark my words, your grasping nature will be the undoing of you. Money is your God, isn't it? Despite everything that is happening to this once great country of ours you still can't see the warning lights. Why do you persist in these reckless demands?'

'Because I haven't been paid for six weeks!' I shout.

'Where do you think the money came from to buy the pantechnicon?' asks Sid.

'That's what I'm complaining about!' I say. 'You fix yourself up with a Japanese movie camera and I—'

'What are you on about?' says Sid. 'Don't you know nothing? A pantechnicon is a furniture van. I've been ploughing back the profits, haven't I? You forgo a bit now so you make much more later. It's standard business practice.'

'Oh,' I say. 'I thought it was that home movie set you were taking all those pictures of your new car with.' Sid rests his arm across my shoulders. 'No, Timmo. Nothing like that. That's a Nikon. I advise you to think very seriously about getting one. You can build up a treasure trove of memories.'

'That's very thoughtful of you, Sid,' I say, allowing a trace of sarcasm to creep into my voice. 'Trouble is, I'm not going to have any memories at this rate.'

'Faith,' says Sid. 'Faith! That's what you lack. Frome

wasn't built in a day, you know. The rewards are always more satisfying when you've had to wait for them. You know what Winston Churchill said?'

'He said a lot of things, Sid.'

'Exactly, Timmo. And you never want to forget it.'

Sid is still rambling on when we pull up outside 17 Wandsworth Gardens, a large semi-detached house near the common.

'I was hoping it would be a little one to start with,' I say. 'How are we going to do it?'

'We'll take all the big stuff out first,' says Sid. 'Then we'll fit the other bits round it.' He flicks out a comb and starts tarting up his barnet. 'Watch how you go, here. Mrs Ripley is a bit special.'

'You've come across her before, have you?' I say.

I don't mean anything by the remark but Sid swings round like I have slapped him in the kisser. 'What have you heard?' he says.

'Nothing, nothing,' I say. 'Don't get your knickers in a twist.'

'Just watch it,' says Sid. 'This lady could do us a lot of good if she likes the way we work. A word from her could find its way into a lot of ears.' He sticks his finger in his cakehole and wipes it along his eyebrows.

I am looking forward to my first brush with the good lady and when the front door opens I am not disappointed. She is small and richly knockered with long dark hair tumbling round her rocks and boulders. Her north and south is a particularly appealing feature because not only is it very handily situated beneath her hooter but it is shaped like a cupid's bow lying on half a grapefruit. A veritable banquet for the snogger. While I let my mince pies run all over her like a couple of of adventurous mice she turns her smouldering orbs on Sid.

'Sidney Noggett, as I live and breathe faster,' she husks. 'It's been a long time.'

Sidney looks uncomfortable – since his trousers are always two sizes too small for him this is not surprising. 'We've come,' he says.

Mrs Ripley turns her eye on me. 'How very flattering,' she says.

'Er – well, yes,' says Sid. 'This is my assistant, Timmy.'

'Partner,' I say firmly. I have had enough of the assistant routine.

'Howdy, partner,' says Mrs Ripley, stepping to one side. 'Mosey into the mansion and start getting to grips with the problem.'

'Everything to go?' says Sid.

'Everything except the double bed. You remember the double bed, Sidney?'

Sid gulps. 'Yes, Mrs Ripley.'

'Maureen, please. Surely we know each other well enough to be on first name terms?'

'Maureen,' says Sid like he is afraid the word might bite him.

'That's better? Would you like a cup of tea now or later?'

'Later, thanks,' says Sid. 'We'll break the back of it first.' With these auspicious words he swings round and knocks down a large vase that is standing on the hall table. It smashes into about a hundred pieces.

If Mrs Ripley is heartbroken she conceals the fact brilliantly. 'Oh look,' she says, plunging into the wreckage. 'Little Ben's Dinky car. He will be pleased.'

'I'm very sorry,' grovels Sid. 'You must let us know how much that cost and we'll come to some sort of arrangement when we settle up.'

'I think Charles paid about three hundred pounds for it,'

she says. 'Don't worry, I never really liked it and I think they're only worth something as a pair.'

'Do you have another one?' says Sid.

I turn in time with Mrs Ripley and my sleeve brushes against something. There is a loud shattering noise.

'Not any more,' says Mrs R cheerfully. 'Look what's inside this one. He's a naughty little boy, isn't he. We take a butchers at about forty furry crusts. 'I'll get a dustpan and brush,' says Sid.

'Don't worry,' says the bird. 'You go upstairs. I'll attend to this. And mind that curtain. It's very easy to catch your foot and –'

If it had been left to me, I would never have put the stuffed owl there in the first place. The curtain pole smashes the glass case and the owl slowly topples forward on to the table and lies on its back with one claw pointing accusingly at Sid.

'That was bloody clumsy of you,' says Sid.

'What do you mean!?' I say. 'It was your foot in the curtain.'

'But you nudged me.'

'Don't worry,' breezes Mrs Ripley. 'If anybody's to blame it's me. I kept meaning to take that damn hem up.' She examines the two-foot rip as Sid removes one of his plates. 'I won't have to bother now.'

'This is terrible!' bleats Sid as we reach the landing. 'We can't afford any more breakages.'

'Mind those little ornaments,' I say.

'What little ornaments?'

'Like the one you're standing on.'

'Oh my gawd!' Sid sweeps up the shattered remains. 'Those little Neasden Shepherdesses are worth a few bob, aren't they?'

'Dresden Shpherdesses,' I say. 'It seems to me they put everything in bloody stupid places in this house.'

Sid shoves the broken bits of the shepherdess in his pocket. 'Yeah. They got to expect a few breakages, haven't they? Still, we must be careful. We don't want to give people the impression that we're slapdash.'

'Absolutely not,' I say, arranging the rest of the ornaments along the shelf so that there is no obvious gap. 'Do you think it's favourite to start at the top?'

'Definitely,' says Sid. 'That way, when we're knackered, we'll be at the bottom and we won't have so far to carry the stuff.'

'On the other hand, if we cleared the stuff at the bottom first, we wouldn't have so much to bump into on the way down.'

'I wish you hadn't said that,' says Sid. 'That smacks of sound reasoning. Now you have me in two minds.'

'You should be grateful for either of them,' I say.

Sid does not care for the tone of that remark and draws back his arm to deliver a clip round the earhole. There is an ugly crunching noise and he turns to see that he has put his elbow through the glass over a picture. 'Now look what you've done!' he says.

'I think it's rather nice,' I say. 'I mean, the way it splinters out like the rays of the rising sun. It is a bit Japanesy, anyway.'

'You're going to get one of my japankneesies in your ballsies if you're not careful!' hisses Sid. 'Pull yourself together for gawd's sake!'

We go into the first room at the top of the stairs and there is an enormous double bed. 'Thank goodness we don't have to move that,' I say.

Sid looks at it with a wistful expression on his mug. 'Yeah,' he says.

'Moved it before, have you?' I say. 'Up and down, perhaps?'

'Don't be disgusting,' says Sid. 'You sully something rare and special when you talk like that. What Maureen and I shared was, well, beautiful. A once-in-a-lifetime experience. Our idol was touched by magic.'

'Your idle what?' I ask.

'Idle nothing, you ignorant twit!' bawls Sid. 'I was referring to our rustic interlude, our I-D-Y-L-L.'

'That's pronounced idyll,' I say. 'Blimey, Sid. It's no wonder people can't understand you.'

'It doesn't matter how it's pronounced,' says Sid impatiently. 'It's the depth of feeling that counts. Oh, Timmo, don't you get it?'

'Now and then,' I say.

'You're so coarse,' sniffs Sid. 'Untouched by higher feelings. Don't you detect that Maureen is different to other women?'

'Not with the naked eye,' I say. 'You've obviously seen more of her than I have.'

Sid shakes his head and closes his eyes despairingly. 'I'm referring to spiritual qualities,' he says. 'Doesn't that woman's fragile innocence break over you in waves?'

'Fragile innocence?' I say. 'You are referring to Big Knockers? I thought she was about as spiritual as a brick chicken house.'

The trouble with Sid is that his stupidity is laced with a strong streak of romanticism. Before he got hitched to my sister Rosie he thought that he was the only thing standing between her and the nunnery. In fact, what Rosie didn't know about the facts of life could be written on a piece of confetti, leaving plenty of room for the manufacturer's name.

'Watch it!' snarls Sid. 'I had something very big going with that woman.'

'It can't be what I'm thinking of, then,' I say. 'Tell me, what was it?'

'You can sneer,' says Sid. 'But there was a time when our relationship seriously threatened the fabric of my marriage to your sister. That's why I had to break it off.'

'I think you broke a bit too much off,' I say. 'You can overdo these things, you know.'

Sid shows no signs of having heard me. 'Must be going on for three years since I last saw her. When we started this lot up I decided to circularise her.'

'You haven't got the training,' I tell him. 'You nearly fainted when they had that commercial for blood donors on the telly. Anyway, you can't do it to women, can you?'

'What are you on about?' says Sid. 'I'm baring my heart to you and all you can do is take the piss. You're not dealing with a scrubber, you know. This woman is class and refinement down to the tips of her toenails. You've never met anything like it so you don't know. Take my word for it, sonny. Maureen makes Barbara Cartland seem like Albert Steptoe in drag.'

'I know what you mean,' I say, thoughtfully. 'She does look a bit funny, doesn't she?'

For a moment I think that Sid is going to belt me. 'Are you talking about Maureen?' he says.

'No, no,' I say. 'Barbara Cartland.'

At that moment, the woman herself walks in carrying a bottle of champagne – I mean Maureen Ripley, not Barbara Cartland. 'Hello,' she says. 'I thought we might have a drink to cheer ourselves up. It's a sad moment moving house, isn't it? What you might call a touching experience.'

So saying, she squeezes Sid's upper thigh – quite a long

way up in fact and veering over towards regions adjacent. It may be unkind of me but I can't help thinking that Sid's impression of Mrs Ripley as being fragile and refined could be a bit exaggerated.

'Oh yes,' says Sid. 'Well, we haven't got very far yet.'

Mrs Ripley swells out her bristols and lightly runs her fingers up Sid's chest. 'That's not like you, Sid. You used to be a fast worker.'

'We're just sizing the job up,' I say, making no secret of the fact that my minces are browsing over the rich pasture of the lady's breasts. 'Shall I open that?'

After a couple of seconds, she realises that I am talking about the champagne and not her lace-up blouse. 'Oh yes,' she says. 'Would you?'

'With the greatest of pleasure,' I say, pouting my tiptoes at her.

As you can see, I have decided that it is time to mesmerise her with the breathless suavity of my *savoire faire*, to say nothing of my *je ne sais quoi*. I have never opened a bottle of champagne before but it must be just like the pomagne stuff we had at Aunty Nora's silver wedding party – where Dad was sick in the window box. All you had to do was unwind the wire and shake it about until the cork began to work loose.

'I'll pop out and get some glasses,' says Mrs R.

Sid can hardly wait till she is through the door before he is on at me. 'Are you trying to prove something?' he says. 'Stop messing about. It's embarrassing.'

'Hang on,' I say. 'Here it comes!'

I do not exaggerate. A froth of champagne sploshes all over the pink eiderdown. If Sid did not act with unusual quick-wittedness and whip a chamber pot out of a bedside cabinet we would be in real trouble.

Maureen Ripley re-enters the room with a tray of

glasses as I stand holding the neck of the bottle over the rim of Sid's po. 'Wouldn't you rather have it out of a glass?' she says.

Sid blushes. 'I'm afraid we had a little accident,' he says. 'My partner is a bit of a berk on the quiet.'

Mrs Ripley looks at the bed. 'Oh dear. Never mind, I expect it will be all right if we leave it to dry. Worse things have happened.' She gives Sid a meaningful glance and, seizing the neck of the champagne bottle between finger and thumb, directs it over her glass. When she has helped herself, she flicks a finger against the froth at the rim of the bottle and licks it. The way she does it sends shivers down the length of my one-eyed trouser snake. If Sid thinks that butter would not melt in this bird's mouth then he should have his hampton examined. I would not reckon on a pound of lard retaining solid shape five seconds after it had passed through her cake hole.

'You want us to leave the bed, don't you?' I say, giving her the famous Lea slow burn.

'You can't leave something you haven't got into, can you?' she says, knowingly. 'Come on, drink up.'

I am strictly a bitter man myself and I find the taste of Mrs Ripley's champagne a lot less to my liking than the pomagne we had at Aunty Nora's knees up – it is not so sweet for one thing. What I will say for it is that it certainly gets you pissed quick. Hardly has the contents of the second glass slipped down my hairy goat than I am feeling decidedly light-headed. I slip out to the karsi for a Swiss Miss and when I return, Mrs Ripley is standing by the window with her arm round Sid's waist.

'I don't know what's the matter with you, Sid,' she is saying. 'You used to be so lively.' She turns to me. 'Your friend here seems to have much more get up and go.' She rubs her hand up and down my Derby Kell and makes 'Grrgh! !' noises.

'Sid lives in the past, sometimes,' I say, throwing in a bit of the old character analysis. It always goes down a treat with the birds. They love raking through their mental make-up boxes.

'I used to be like that, once,' says the lovely Mrs R. 'Then I started living for the future. Now, it's the present every time. "Do it now", that's my motto.' She tosses back the rest of her glass of champagne and bites me on the chest. Yes, just like that. It quite takes my breath away.

'Has your husband got the day off for the move?' says Sid in a strained voice.

Maureen nods. 'He's waiting at Peterborough. There's no one going to interrupt us here. Oooooooh! Just think what we could get up to.'

A number of possibilities are occurring to me and it seems not beyond the wilder realms of speculation that a spot of group activity should feature amongst them. Whilst never loath to dish it out amongst a bevy of bints I am less enthusiastic about playing slot the gopher when the teams are unequally weighted in the male's favour. However, in this instance, maybe I should reconsider my position – or positions, you never know your luck. The continuing presence of Maureen Ripley in Sid's excuse for a mind is clearly a threat to the stability of my sister's marriage. If I can help lay the ghost of the past and prove to Sid that Mrs R is not what he has cracked her up to be then I will be striking an important blow for the cause of family unity. At the very least I will be getting my end away which can't be bad.

'Do you think we ought to take the eiderdown off the bed?' I say.

'Just fold it back,' says Mrs Ripley giving me a highly naughty look.

'I don't think it's gone through,' I say.

Mrs Ripley scrambles on to the bed and hauls her knockers over the spot where any stain would be likely to show itself. From where I am standing you could post early for Christmas in her cleavage. 'It's all right,' she says. 'There's nothing there.'

This is not a remark that could be made about the front of my overall. It is standing room only at crutch level.

Mrs R runs her tongue over her lips and slides her legs down the bed so that her skirt rides up to her thighs. If this was not enough to put your hampton on purple alert she lies back against the pillow and pats the bed beside her. 'It's very soft,' she says.

One of the few things that is, I think to myself as I glance across at Sid. He looks like a man under strain and is fiddling nervously with the stem of his empty champagne glass. So nervously that it breaks in two. Maureen Ripley gives him what might be described as a melting look. 'You don't know your own strength, do you, Sidney?' she says.

Sid gulps. 'I'm sorry. I don't know what's come over me.'

'Well, it certainly won't be me at this rate', sniffs Mrs R, turning to me. 'Do you want to test the posture springing, Chu-Chi Face?'

It seems like an offer nobody could refuse and when Mrs Ripley stretches out her hand I sink down on the bed like heavy dust. Hardly have I dented the upholstery than Mrs R has puckered up her cakehole trimming and is directing it unerringly towards my own fair lips. She rolls over against me and her body seems to be touching mine at about half a dozen different places.

'Kiss me!!' she says like Barbra Streisand finding that the last train leaves town in five minutes.

I don't have time to consider the suggestion because she has launched herself on to my lips like they are a couple of fat, pink mice about to take refuge behind my teeth, and she is a starving moggy.

'Ah hem,' says Sid. 'It's time we got down to it, I think, Timmo.'

I don't answer him for obvious reasons and marvel at the practised ease with which Mrs R whips out my dick. It reminds me of my Uncle Norbert filleting a kipper – not, I hasten to add, that there is anything unwholesome about Uncle Norbert – apart from the fact that he only changes his socks when England win the World Cup.

'There's work to be done,' says Sid uncomfortably. 'I can't do it all by myself, you know.'

Mrs Ripley rises swiftly to her knees and proceeds to unzip her skirt. I pull it down and get on with removing my own clothing. The bed is bouncing up and down like a trampoline. Anybody coming through the door would think that it was some kind of party game with Sid as the referee. Mrs R's Manchesters are really jumbo numbers and it is not surprising that she lies on the bed once she has slung her tit sling. If she caught herself under the chin with one of them, it could do a lot of damage. Once her shoulders are against the sheets, she arches her back and invites me to remove her panties. Not with any words but with a quick wriggle of her hips. I am down to the Y-fronts by this time and percy is trying to prise them off by himself. He has climbed over the rim and is exerting strong downward leverage. Mrs R is not slow to play the US Cavalry and her helpful fingers allow my action man kit to lunge forward like one of those cannon at the Tower of London.

I peel off her panties and we are both starkers and waiting for the off – or, more appropriately, on.

It is at about this time that I am conscious of the sound of heavy breathing coming from neither Maureen nor myself. As percy commences his journey into the interior and Mrs R closes her fingers tightly round my sit feature, I turn my head and catch a glimpse of Sid hopping round the room trying to pull his trousers over his shoes. It is only a glimpse because he topples backwards and disappears from view accompanied by the sound of breaking furniture.

'Join us when you can, Sidney,' says Mrs R, baring her teeth. 'There's no hurry.'

'I'll be right with you,' pants Sid. 'Just as soon as I've got my foot out of this bleeding potty!'

CHAPTER EIGHT

In which Timmy and Sid find that they have been duped and are forced to take evasive action from a betrayed husband.

Now it is not often that I can be accused of reticence – mainly because I can say, with complete justification, that I have no idea what it means – but our session with Mrs Maureen – 'More in than out' – Ripley is another matter. You would not cocoa some of the things that go on. I hardly know where to put myself when I think about it – mind you, I hardly knew where to put myself at the time. Once Sid joined the party, space became at a premium so to speak. Upstairs, downstairs and in my lady's chamber – well, not in her chamber because Sid broke it getting it off his foot. That wasn't the only thing either. The bed was in a terrible state by the time we rolled off it. I could understand why she didn't want to take it with her.

I can remember standing there trying to pull on Sid's trousers and thinking 'Oh my gawd! We've been through all that and we haven't even started work yet!' I am so knackered that I nearly fall asleep putting my socks on. That is another thing the experience teaches me. I had always wondered why those blokes in the dirty photographs never took their Brightons off. Now I know. It is so they don't have to bend down to pull them on afterwards.

Sid is in a worse condition than me, if anything, and it is Mrs Ripley's furniture that suffers. You could fill a sack with the chips off some of the heavier articles and the noise when we go through the hall is like an army marching on egg shells – there are that many breakages lying about. As for the walls – on tight corners they look as if they have been attacked with an axe and on the stairs you would think someone had run a rake down the wall paper. Every time we go through the front door for another load I mutter 'Never again!' and I know Sid agrees with me though he doesn't say anything – he can't say anything, poor sod. The remarkable thing is the way Mrs Ripley tolerates it all. I know that she has had a few glasses of champagne and that birds perk up after a spot of in and out – spot? It was more like a bleeding epidemic – but she is like a little ray of sunshine dancing about.

'Don't bother to sweep anything up,' she says when we have got the last tea chest of china aboard. 'I'll look after that. You wouldn't fancy another glass of champagne, would you?'

Sid and I lock shoulders in the door. What a woman! It is just as well that she is making her own way to Peterborough. I can imagine what a journey with her would be like. At least, I think to myself, Sid will have been cured of his romantic delusions. Lea the exorcist has done his tiny bit to preserve family unity.

'No doubt you noticed a change?' I say grimly as Sid eases the van into first gear.

'In Maureen?' says Sid. 'No, not particularly. She was always gay and vivacious.'

I don't say any more after that – I mean, what can you say? Sid would probably reckon that Attila the Hun was a dead ringer for Tiny Tim on a horse.

The journey to Peterborough is a nightmare. Not because of the road but because of our condition. We are both falling asleep before we hit the A1. I suggest that Sid keeps his window open and hangs his arm out of it so that the wind rushes up his sleeve and keeps him awake. Sid reckons that he would be better off hanging his leg out of the window. He actually tries it, but finds that he has to steer with his right arm underneath his leg. It is possible but does not give you quite the freedom of movement recommended by the Highway Code. In the end he packs it in because he is worried about getting his dick perished. I reckon that mine perished on that bed with Mrs Ripley.

It is just getting dark when we reach Peterborough and I am not looking forward to our meeting with Mr Ripley. For one thing, I am going to have difficulty looking him in the eye, and for another, he has probably been expecting us for the last three hours. I hope he is not the impatient type.

'Here we are,' says Sid. 'Number eighty.'

'Are you sure?' I say. 'It's much smaller than the last place.'

'So much the better,' says Sid. 'We won't have so far to carry the stuff, will we?'

'There's no lights on,' I say. 'I hope there's somebody there.'

'There must be,' says Sid. 'Come on.' Sid is always more hopeful than me when disaster beckons. As we toddle up the garden path I have a nasty feeling that all is not well, Sid rings the front door bell and nothing happens.

'It is ringing is it?' I say.

Sid presses his head against the door. 'I can't hear anything,' he says.

'Try pressing the door bell while you're listening,' I say. Sid looks as if he is going to say something and then does as I suggest. 'Yeah, I can hear it,' he says. 'He must have popped out for a moment.' He listens again and the door clicks open as he leans against it.

'Might as well have a shufti,' I say. 'Maybe he's left a note.'

'I'm surprised that Maureen isn't here,' says Sid.

'Maybe half a dozen blokes arrived to disconnect the electricity,' I say.

Sid does not say anything but pushes open the front door. 'Blimey!' he says. 'It's already furnished.'

I look over his shoulder and see a hallstand, mirror, table, carpets, the lot. 'We must have the wrong house,' I say.

Sid shakes his head in amazement. 'I could have sworn this was the address.'

We tramp down to the gate and check the number.

'It is the address,' says Sid.

'Maybe there's two roads with the same name,' I say.

'There can't be. We'd better have another look inside. Maybe it's only the hall that's furnished.'

'I don't like the sound of this, I say. 'I've got one of my feelings.'

'Shut up!' says Sid. 'You're always on about something.'

He leads the way into the house and wipes his feet on the doormat. 'Let's try and get everything right, this time,' he says. 'No mess ups.'

I don't say anything but wipe my feet and open the door of what turns out to be the lounge. 'You couldn't get a copy of the TV Times in here,' I say. 'It's chockablock.'

Sid takes a gander at the room full of furniture and a worried expression comes over his face. 'There's something funny going on,' he says, like a kid watching Santa Claus climb into bed with his mum.

'There could be a flat upstairs, I suppose,' I say.

'We'd never get that wardrobe up those stairs,' says Sid.

'We could if we took it apart a bit more.'

'We weren't supposed to take it apart in the first place!' says Sid, heatedly 'Gordon Bennett. What are we going to do?'

'Better take a look upstairs,' I say.

We have just got to the landing, when a door opens and a bird sticks her head round it. Her hair is all over the place and she looks rumpled in more ways than one.

'Mr Ripley?' says Sid.

The bird looks surprised, as well she might. 'What do you want?' she says.

'We're the removal men,' I say. 'I'm sorry if we disturbed you but nobody answered the bell and the door was open.'

'Removal men?!' says the bird. 'I'm not moving anywhere.'

'We know you're not,' says Sid. 'We've brought the stuff.'

'What stuff?' says the bird.

Sid clears his throat and I get another of my nasty feelings. 'The furniture from Wandsworth Gardens.'

'WHAT?' The exclamation comes from the interior of the bedroom and is followed by the appearance of a middle-aged geezer wearing a pair of trousers with his shirt half tucked into them.

'Ah, Mr Ripley,' says Sid in his most 'pleased to meet you' manner. 'Your furniture is without. Where would you like it?'

'Back in my fucking house!' says the bloke. 'Who the hell told you to bring it up here?'

'Your wife,' says Sid. 'We were hired to assist in the movement of your goods and chattels to your new abode.'

'New abode?' says the bloke. 'I haven't got a new abode. This house belongs to my part-time secretary. I stop in here sometimes to give her a bit of dictation. I do a lot of business in the midlands.'

'A very satisfactory arrangement, I'm sure,' says Sid, gazing past the bird now revealed in her transparent black negligee to the crumpled bed with the large Teddy Bear sitting on it. 'Am I to understand, then, that there has been some kind of misunderstanding?'

'There's been no misunderstanding!' snarls the bloke. 'If you're telling the truth, it looks as if my wife has been playing some kind of stupid practical joke.'

'Oh dear,' says Sid. 'What do you suggest we do?'

'I've already made my suggestion,' says the bloke unpleasantly. 'Get the stuff back to my home where it belongs!' I can see this bloke as a captain of industry. Add water and you would have instant shit.

'But we haven't got paid yet,' I bleat.

Ripley remains unmoved. 'That's your lookout,' he says. 'You want to be more careful about the kind of work you take on.'

Sid looks at me and we exchange what might be described as an emphatic nod. 'We're going to get paid for this job,' he says grimly. 'If you think otherwise, we'll dump your stuff in the front garden. Right, Timmo?'

'Right, Sid,' I say.

We move towards the door waiting for the sound of Ripley's voice. 'Hang on a minute. Tell you what I'll do. I can see that you've been put to a bit of bother. You take the stuff back and I'll pay you for the journey up here. After all, you haven't had to unload it.'

'I'd better get on with that shorthand you gave me, Mr Ripley,' says the bird patting her hair and trying to appear dead nonchalant.

'He gave you a short hand as well, did he?' says Sid. 'You might take something down for me some time.'

Mr Ripley does not care for the tone of that remark and I am not sorry that he does not travel with us on the way back to Wandsworth Gardens.

'I reckon he'll kill her, don't you?' says Sid. 'I wouldn't

half belt Rosie if she ever did anything like that.'

'Why do you think she did it, Sid?' I ask.

'It's obvious, isn't it? She found out he was having a bit on the side and thought she'd clobber him in his love nest. It's funny when you think about it. Imagine how that bird would have reacted if she'd been on her tod when we rolled up.'

'Highly jocular,' I say. 'But it seems a bit like cutting off your hampton to spite your cobblers, to me. What is his wife going to do without any furniture?'

'Women never think about things like that, Timmo,' says Sid wisely. 'Poor little thing, I expect she was distraught.'

I look at him closely but I think he is serious.

It is funny, but though I was dead knackered on the way to Peterborough, I feel much better on the way back. I must have found a second wind from somewhere. Sid, if the niff in the cab is anything to go by. We get back to Wandsworth Gardens at half past ten and Ripley's car is parked outside with steam pouring out of the radiator. He must have nearly done himself an injury rushing back home.

'We'd better see what the form is, hadn't we?' I say, starting up the path.

'Hang on,' says Sid. 'Don't go without something. We've got to organise our remaining resources of energy. Give us a hand with this settee.'

We have just lugged the thing up to the house when the front door flies open. Standing there, shaking with helpless fury, is Mr Ripley. 'Was this place like this when you left?' he shouts.

'Like what?' says Sid.

'Look!'

We leave the settee and go into the hall.

'Blimey!' says Sid.

The walls look like someone has tried to imitate the writing in the piss house of The Highwayman. There are some very rude words about, all of them drawn with a lipstick. 'I never knew you spelt it like that,' says Sid.

'It's the way she does her Ks,' I say.

'Upstairs it's even worse,' sobs Mr R. 'I don't know what could have come over her.' I try not to look at Sid.

'How could the bed have got like that?'

'The bed?' says Sid. 'Oh, the bed. Yes.'

'It was all right when we left,' I say.

'That's right,' says Sid. 'Has something happened to it?'

'It's shattered,' says Ripley sounding as if he isn't in such good nick himself. 'She left this note, he continues. 'I can't bring myself to read it.'

'I'll read it,' says Sid cheerfully. Even as he stretches out his hand I feel that he is making a big mistake.

'Maybe, Mr Ripley doesn't want –' I begin, but Sid waves me down, and rips open the envelope.

' "Dear Pig-face –" ' Sid smiles confidentially at Ripley. 'It's for you.' Ripley clenches his fists but Sid is continuing to read. ' "– if you want to know why the bed collapsed, I suggest you ask the two –" '

'Yes?' says Ripley. 'The two what?'

Sid tries to crumple the note up. 'It's too harrowing,' he says. 'It was clearly written while the balance of the woman's mind was overdrawn.'

'Give me that!' Ripley snatches the note from Sid's hand and starts to devour it with his eyes.

Sid nods towards the door desperately. 'Run for it!'

We are neck and neck as we thunder down the stairs and out through the front door. 'Stay where you are, you swines. I'm going to kill you!'

With Ripley shouting things like that, there is no incentive to hang around and Sid and I are clearing the garden gate as Ripley hits the crazy paving – literally, as it turns out. Mr R does not know about the settee parked outside the front door and takes an Oliver Hardy over the top of it. Come to think of it, I don't think the path had crazy paving until he landed. I start to scramble into the cab but Sid pulls me back.

'Leave it!' he says. 'We'll never get it started in time.'

He starts to run up the street and I go after him. If this is what being a removal man is all about I reckon we would be better off sticking to road haulage.

CHAPTER NINE

In which Timmy calls on a northern club and finds himself pressed into service by an all-female audience when the male strip-tease artist fails to put in an appearance.

'That's funny,' says Sid, pushing the paper across to me me. 'Look at that.'

It is next morning and we are having a quick cuppa in the caff prior to picking up the van.

'Yeah. One of them's a bit bigger than the other one, isn't it?' I say.

'Not the bird's tits, you berk! I'm talking about the lead story "Furniture van burns to ashes in suburban street".'

'What!' I snatch back the paper. 'By the cringe! That's ours, isn't it? I recognise the number.' In fact, the buckled number plate is about the only means of telling that the twisted pile of metal was a vehicle. 'Yeah, look! It says Wandsworth Gardens in the write-up.'

'No! I can't believe it,' says Sid. 'All your wages were tied up in that van. How could it have happened?'

'It says here it was empty,' I say. Sid looks at me. I look at Sid. 'He couldn't.'

'He has,' says Sid. 'What a mean, twisted bastard.'

'Not to mention that rotten bitch, Maureen,' I say.

Sid is swift to take jumbo-sized umbrage. 'What are you on about?' he says. 'This act of arson reveals the twisted mentality of the man she was married to.'

'She was a bit twisted herself, wasn't she?' I say. 'Dragging us into bed like that.'

'That was a cry for help,' says Sid as if explaining something to a child. 'Your knowledge of fundamental physiology isn't worth a kick up the khyber, is it?'

'You must be soft in the nut,' I say. 'That Maureen was a very no, no lady. Why did she want to drop us in it with her old man if she was so blooming nice?'

'Integrity,' says Sid. 'She couldn't live a lie. Feeling as she did towards me, she realised that it made a mockery of her relationship with her husband. She had to tell him. I think that shows real courage.'

'Feeling as she did towards *you*? What about me?'

Sid puts on his humouring smile again. 'She was using you to get at me, don't you see? She could sense that I was paralysed by nostalgia. She flirted with you in order to bring me up short.'

'That's certainly the way you came up,' I say. 'She has a lot to answer for, doesn't she?'

'It doesn't matter what you say,' says Sid. 'I'll always have a soft spot for that woman.'

'I noticed that, too,' I say. 'Like a steamed-up pyjama tassle. You want to take a course of iron tablets.' Not for the first time, Sid is swift to demonstrate that he is very short in the sense of humour department and we leave on bad terms. Sid is bird-brained in more ways than one. Not only is he an idiot but he has a bird's ability to create an explanation for any sequence of events that bears no relation to the real facts and absolves him from any responsibility or blame. In this case, he genuinely believes that arch scrubber Maureen is as pure as driven Omo – stupid, isn't it?

Of course, old man Ripley says that he knows nothing about the furniture van burning down and refuses to pay anything towards the expense of the Peterborough trip. He says that since his wife ordered it, she can pay for it. Unfortunately, despite her insane infatuation for Sidney, the lady has done a bunk and is not available for comment.

Sid is most upset and I am not totally surprised when someone nicks a precast cement lorry, breaks open a window on Ripley's car, and tops it up with quick-drying cement. I believe that Ripley gets a very nasty surprise when he sets off for the office in the morning. What is more, he can't find anyone to move the car. It looks as if it will have to stay outside his house for ever. Who could have done such a thing remains a mystery though Sid does have a lot of trouble getting the cement out from under his finger nails.

With the furniture van gone for a burton, it is back to the road haulage and a very strange experience in the north of England. I have been signed up to take a load of glasses to a working men's club at a place called Barnly – apparently they go through quite a lot of glasses up there – and I am on a bonus for prompt delivery. As always happens on this kind of occasion I hit more snags than a hedgehog trying to have it off with a pin cushion and by the time I cross the border into Lancashire I am an hour behind schedule. It has been pissing with rain and one of the motorway lanes has been closed for repairs over a five mile period – I reckon they must make these motorways out of sponge cake. I gaze ahead into the deepening gloom and see a lorry that has pulled up on the hard shoulder. Beside it is a familiar figure. Long fur coat, high heeled boots, shoulder length hair sprouting out from under a Dick Whittington titfer with a feather through it. It is Shirl. She waggles a thumb and my foot goes down on the brake pedal before I can tell it to mind its own business.

'Can you take me away from all thees?' she says.

'I'm going to Barnly,' I say. 'Is the gaffer all right?'

She follows my nod towards the other lorry. 'It depends what you mean by all right.'

'Yeah,' I say, deciding that it is favourite not to ask for

further information. 'Get in if you're coming. I'm late.'

She clambers in beside me and I make sure that I clock a long gander at her pins. I am mighty partial to the sight of birds giving a trailer for the main feature as they get in and out of vehicles.

'You don't remember me, do you?' I say.

She doesn't even look at me. 'I make it a point never to remember anyone. Life's easier like that.'

'You get around,' I say. 'I've seen you a few times.'

'Yes,' she says. She is clearly not a great conversationalist, this bird

'I suppose you travel from one public speaking contest to another.'

'Very funny.' Her expression tells me that she's lying. 'Come to think of it, I do recognise you. You were carrying a load of fertiliser, weren't you? I thought I recognised the smell.'

'Blimey. It's not still hanging about, is it?'

'The smell of your after shave – only it can't be after shave, can it?'

'Cologne,' I say. The truth is that I have started growing a beard. Sid takes the piss, of course, but I reckon that it rather suits me. They are dead fashionable at the moment, aren't they? I reckon that it brings out the artistic side of my nature yet at the same time emphasises my brutish masculinity. It also saves on razor blades. Dad is dead choked because he had a special use for all my old razor blades – shaving. He is so mean that he used to hang the tear-off calendar in the karsi – until one June morning when he ate too many prunes and took us through to December 23 at one sitting.

'I always used to think that it was "Odour Cologne" meaning "pong" rather than "Eau de Cologne" meaning "water of",' I say, conversationally. 'It's funny that, isn't it?'

Shirl looks at me and shakes her head. 'You're barmy,' she says. I don't think that she has been exposed to my kind of breathless suavity before. It does come as a shock to a lot of girls. They don't know how to react. 'I don't think I've had sex with a bearded bloke,' she says.

'You wouldn't be able to remember anyway, would you?' I say, a bit sarcastic-like.

'Maybe not.' There is a long pause and I reckon that the subject has been dropped. 'It depends what it was like,' she says, thoughtfully. I can feel her looking at me expectantly and goose pimples pepper my thighs. If I was not over an hour late I could be very interested in the way she delivered her last remark.

'Uhm,' I say. 'I suppose it does, really.'

'I mean, it could be quite nice. There must be lots of things you could do with a furry beard.' She shifts her position so that she has turned towards me. Her legs part slightly and she runs a hand along the inside of her thigh. The lorry behind hoots as I pull out without looking in my mirror.

'Where are you spending the night?' I say.

'That depends. I haven't made any plans.'

'I've got to deliver these glasses,' I say, nodding over my shoulder. 'Maybe when I've done it we could—'

'Pull over.'

'Why? What's the matter?'

'You are. You and my feelings. Sometimes I get it very bad for a feller. Very bad and very sudden. Pull over, I want you inside me.'

She runs one of her hands over my beard and then down my chest and— 'Wow!' I nearly drive over a Volkswagen like it is a humpback bridge.

'I can't pull over,' I say. 'It's against the law and I'm late as it is. I only stopped because it was you. Can't we get together when I've done the job? I can buy you some supper—'

'No! I want it now. It won't be the same later.'

Oh dear. Once again, I find myself on the horn of a Dali Lama. Duty calling in one lughole while my cream-thighed love goddess croons in the other. What would you do? Yes, me too!

'I can only stop for a minute,' I say, slamming on the anchors and steering for the hard shoulder. 'My partner would kill me if he knew I was doing this.'

'You don't have to tell him. I know men who would give their right arm to do what you're going to be doing in a minute.'

Hardly have I pulled on the hand brake before she has raised her back bumpers and tugged her drawers and tights down to knee level. Percy is probing the stratosphere and all seems set for a bout of instant cock snuffing. Then I look in the driving mirror. A cop car is sliding to a halt behind us. Even as I watch it jerk to a halt, the doors open and two bules get out.

'Fuzz!' I say.

'That's right,' says Shirl poking me playfully in the balls. 'Haven't you got any?'

'I mean cops!' I say. Shirl's knicks shoot up faster than the cost of living.

'What do you think you're doing?' the cop appears to be staring at my crutch but I try and believe that it is just my guilty conscience.

'The engine was overheating,' I say. 'I thought I'd better pull off for a while.'

'You want to watch it. You'll stunt your growth.' The

second cop laughs to see such fun. He has a big, black bushy beard.

'Hello,' says the first cop. 'Look who's here. It's Shirl. What are you up to?'

'I'm up to page seven of *Little Women*,' says my companion. 'What are you up to?'

'What a wonderful sense of humour,' says the cop. 'You ought to be on the telly.'

The second cop sticks his mug through the window and I feel Shirl perk up as she clocks his beard. I must say, it has more promise than mine if you go for the door mat variety. Real 'Sixteen men on a dead man's chest' stuff.

'Where are you bound for?' he says.

'Nowhere in particular.'

'We'll give you a lift there.'

I would not mind so much if the first cop did not start rubbing his hands together before she has even got out of the cab.

'And you,' he says, turning to me viciously. 'Watch it! We won't be so easy on you next time.'

'Sorry about this,' says Shirl. 'But you can't resist an invitation from the boys in blue, can you?'

The bloke with the beard opens the back door for her and they exchange a look that would unseal an envelope. She does wave as they pull out but I don't reply. Sometimes, I hate coppers.

By the time I have turned off the motorway at Chorley and taken the wrong turning I am an hour and a half late and harassed – very harassed. I know the underside of Sid's armpit better than the country around here. Barnly is a long sprawling town and the Working Men's Club appears to be well hidden. The only action is round an enormous modern building with a commissionaire standing outside. It is picked out in floodlights and an impressive array of motor cars are dropping expensively dressed men and women outside the front door. I imagine that it must be the Town Hall and that the Mayor is holding some kind of function.

'Excuse me, mate,' I say to the geezer on the door. 'Do you know where the Working Men's Club is?'

'Certainly,' says the bloke in a very posh voice. 'Your vehicle is standing in front of it.'

'You're kidding!' I say. 'This place? It's like the Festival Hall.'

'Slightly bigger,' says the bloke clapping his white-gloved hands together against the cold. 'I used to go there a lot in the old days. Evening sir.' He touches his cap to a little old man who goes through the door carrying a whippet under his arm. 'That chap used to sweep out under my machines.'

'Your machines?' I say.

The man nods. 'I used to own a mill round here. It was a luxury I can no longer afford. The wheel has turned full circle. We are the workers, now. Good evening madam.'

The old bird sweeping through with her mate takes no notice of him. They both look like Gary Glitter in drag and they must have robbed a Christmas tree for most of the stuff they're wearing.

'It better be better than last time,' says one of them. 'You expect to see everything, don't you?'

'We won't see anything if we don't get a move on,' says the friend. 'You know how they hog the front rows.'

They disappear through the swing doors and I turn my attention to the commissionaire who is carefully fitting a freshly discovered fag end into a bulging match box.

'Deliveries round the back?' I ask.

He nods. 'Mind you don't scratch the catering manager's Rolls.'

'Why? Does the pastry crack up?' It is only after I have driven off that I realise what he meant. I do feel a fool.

I park Enid and go into the kitchens which are full of blokes shoving handfuls of scampi and chips on to cold plates. They don't seem at all interested in my glasses and I am told to look for someone called Mr Brownlow. Out of the kitchens and along a corridor until I come to another door with a glass panel in it. I look through it and see a load of blokes and birds sitting at tables which stretch for about half a mile until they reach a stage. On the stage is a bloke singing through a microphone. Coming towards the door is a worried looking bloke in a dinner jacket being pursued by a small man wearing a dirty white shirt with a clip-on bow tie – I know it is a clip-on because only one side is attached to the collar.

'If he wants brandy and tomato juice, let him have it,' says Dinner Jacket.

'Flambéd over a chocolate ice cream?' says the little bloke.

'Ah hem. Mr Brownlow?' I say.

'Yes.'

'I'm sorry I'm late. I—'

Brownlow grabs my arm and starts pulling me down the corridor. 'Thank God you've come. You came by road, I suppose?'

'Well – yes.'

'You should have come by train. Another five minutes and they would have ripped the place apart.'

I can imagine the scene. Everybody waiting for a drink and nothing to drink it out of. 'It's all outside,' I say.

'What is?'

'The glasses,' I say.

'Glasses?' Mr Brownlow looks at me in a very funny way.

'You don't want glasses. They wouldn't like it with glasses. It may go down all right in London but it wouldn't up here. Nothing sophisticated up here. That beard's going it a bit. No, you can forget about the glasses.'

Before I can ask him what he is talking about, Mr Brownlow stops outside a door. Through it I can hear what sounds like a female choir singing 'Why are we waiting?' Something tells me there is more to the Barnly Working Men's Club than meets the eye. Could it be that I am poised on the verge of a misunderstanding?

'Do you want to change?' says Mr Brownlow, his hand on the doorknob.

'I've got the overall in the cab,' I say, a bit puzzled.

'Cab?' says Mr B. 'You came all the way from London in a cab? Still, I suppose it's not surprising on the money I'm paying you. What I can't understand is the overall. They won't like that either. They're kinky for sequins up here.'

I take a deep breath. 'Listen Mr Brownjob,' I say. 'I think there's been a—'

'It's Brownlow and you'd best forget about the overall. Where's your music?'

'Music?'

'You must have music!'

'Well, there's a radio in the cab.'

Brownlow strikes his fists against his head in exasperation. 'By gum but you're a rum 'un! I don't know what they're going to make of you. You do it to patter, do you?'

'Patter?' I say.

The sound of 'Why are we waiting' is joined by the uneven stamping of feet. Brownlow tightens his grip on the door knob. 'We can't wait any longer,' he says. 'You'll have to go on as you are. The panic button is on the right of the bongos.'

I don't have time to ask him what the hell he is talking about because he pulls open the door and pushes me through. At first I think I am in the big hall I caught a glimpse of earlier but I soon see that this room is much smaller. There is a small stage in the middle of it and a lot of tables with birds sitting at them – in fact, the only bloke I can see is standing helplessly on the stage. Brownlow gives him a thumbs up sign and he immediately extends an arm towards me. 'Here we are! Here we are! I said we wouldn't let you down, ladies. Better late than never I'm certain you will agree—' I turn towards the door but it is closed. There is no sign of Brownlow – 'We've had a lot of firsts at the Barnly WMC: we were the first to bring you Hughie Green wrestling alligators in foam, the first to bring you the now nationally televised football supporters' club toilet roll throwing competition and, from your point of view the most important of all, the first to bring you male striptease for a purely female audience—'

As the true import of those word sinks in, my blood turns to water. A glance at these birds tells you that they do not spend a lot of time knitting ear muffs for budgies. And they have been drinking, too. The tables are littered with empty stout bottles. Oh my gawd! How am I going to get out?

On the stage, the M.C.'s voice drones on. 'Just a polite reminder, ladies. Please don't touch the artiste—'

The nearest old bag to me, sinks her talons into my thigh. 'Hello, luv,' she croons. She gives me a wink and one of her false eyelashes drops in her Babycham. 'Booger!' she says.

'– the shadow of legal action still hangs over the club after last month's incident. High spirits are one thing, but biting police dogs is something completely different.'

'Get on with it!' shouts an impatient voice and there is an ugly rumble of agreement.

'Now, if you've all ordered your drinks—' Some swing doors burst open and three waiters appear carrying trays loaded with booze. In what seems like seconds, the trays have been emptied and one of the waiters has lost his trousers '– all males will leave the room, the doors will be sealed, and you, ladies, will be able to enjoy Mr Show-All's act in privacy and seclusion.'

'Give us a kiss,' says an old biddy who looks like Liberace's mum. I smile nervously and step into an unorthodox handshake from a bird who must be able to strip the tyres off a ten ten lorry with her bare hands.

'Ladies and ladies. I give you Mr Show-All!!'

I am still bent double as I approach the platform. The MC passes me going like a rocket. Even the waiters are running. 'Good luck, chum,' mutters the MC. 'Don't inflame them too much. The panic button is—'

'By the bongos,' I gasp. 'Yeah, I know.'

Suddenly, I feel very much alone. The doors slam with an echoing sound like you get when you close a vault – you know, you close vaults all the time, don't you – and the lights go down. I can see the ornamental bits round the birds' specs glinting in the darkness. That one over there looks a bit like – no, it couldn't be her, could it? Still, you never know. She might be doing a spot of research. Trying to find something else to complain about.

'Come on. Show us your muscles!' There is a burst of laughter and somebody knocks a glass over.

I take a deep breath. 'You're not going to believe this—'

'Why? Have you got a big one?' More laughter and shouts of 'Get 'em off!'

'I like the beard.'

'Come and tickle my fancy!'

'I'm not what you think I am,' I say desperately.

'He's one of those!' Everybody screams with laughter.

'We'll straighten you out, luv.'

'Off! Off! Off!'

They are stamping again. What am I going to do? If I make a run for it, they'll cut me down before I get to the doors. If I do get to the doors, they are locked. There is only one thing for it: 'Give me the moonlight, give me the girl, and leave the rest to—' I start humming and begin to slide my tank top off my left shoulder. I don't half feel a berk! What's more, I get a crick in my neck. I wouldn't fancy doing this for a living. I wonder where the real Mr Show-All is? Show-All. Does that mean I'm supposed to strip to the buff?

'Get on with it!'

'Leave him alone. He's being artistic, isn't he?'

I am touched that the lady springing to my defence should have noticed. I am also touched by a lady who springs on to the stage and runs her hand up the inside of my leg. I can't do anything about it because both my arms are trapped in the tank top I am struggling to pull off behind my back. At least she is gentle. Not like the one on the way to the stage. By the time I have got an arm free, the groper has returned to her seat, cackling. Trying to keep my cool, I swing the jacket round and round with one hand while popping open the buttons on my shirt with the other. Judging by the sound of squeals and breaking glass, this is a very popular manoeuvre.

'Come on! Show us what you've got!'

'Let it all hang out!'

'Get your drawers off!'

Somehow or other, I have got to spin this out. Who knows? Help may arrive. Perhaps, even, the real Mr Show-

All. I would hate to steal his thunder. Very slowly, I begin to slide my shirt off my shoulders and pull it down my chest.

'Show us your nipples!'

'Get your trousers off.'

'Leave him alone, he knows what he's doing!'

'You shut your mouth!'

'You try and make me!'

One of the ladies by the stage rises to her feet and years of experience suggest to me that she is not about to go to the karsi. A bunch of fives up the bracket is more likely what she has in mind.

'Relax, ladies,' I say, deciding to adapt the role of Timothy the Peacemaker. 'Perhaps I could ask you to assist me in my performance?' I make each of the birds cop hold of a cuff and swivel round so that they can pull off my shirt like it is a skin. Though I say so myself, it is highly artistic and there is a satisfied 'Oooooh' from the audience.

Now I am down to jeans, socks and underpants. If I was that bloke who can make his muscles jump about like he has a clockwork mouse under his skin, I might be able to hold them off for a bit longer, but I am not. When I flex my arms, the only thing that moves is the second hand on my wrist watch.

'Get 'em down!!'

Now I know how the Christians must have felt when they heard the crowd roaring in the arena. There is a very ugly glint in some of the eyes I can see out there. I don't know what they get at home apart from the housekeeping money but it does not seem to be sufficient to satisfy appetites not catered for in the Marguerite Patten Cookery Book.

One thing I must be careful to do is take off my shoes

and socks before my trousers. Not only because it looks prettier but because I don't want to fall flat on my mug like Sid in Maureen Ripley's bedroom. It is very easy to look a bit of a berk when you are hopping round the room with your trousers trapped over your heel.

'Come and sit on my lap, luv.' The lady is swift to spot my predicament – amongst other things. Hardly have I settled on her boney knees than she is having a go at my action man kit. 'What colour pants have you got on?' she says.

'All kinds, I expect,' says her mate, knowingly. 'You remember that other feller? He had forty-six pairs. All transparent. Everyone in the room took a pair off and there were three left over.'

It occurs to me that in my case, forty-odd ladies could be disappointed. Now I am not even certain that I have a pair on. I must have, yet, somehow, I can't feel them. Someone who can feel them is one of the other birds at the table. She shoves her mit down the front of my jeans like it is a lucky dip.

'Hang on!' I say.

For a moment, I think she is taking me literally. I would not mind so much if her hands were not colder than an Eskimo's arsehole. She is not gentle, either. I reckon she must size mangel wurzels for a living. In the end it is necessary for me to change laps in order to rescue percy from a fate worse than poking a power drive potato peeler.

I get one shoe off and then manage to foul up the knot on the other one. The birds all love this because they reckon it is a bit of a tease. Little do they know. At least I am wearing a clean pair of socks. That is something they ought to be thankful for.

'Please!' I say to the bint who is currently trying to expand the nature of the entertainment. 'Remember what the man said: don't touch the goodies!'

'They have to say that,' says the bird. 'They wouldn't get a licence otherwise. Once the doors are locked, they don't care what happens. You can do what you like.'

Not with the doors locked I can't, I think to myself. Gordon Bennett! These women are so cock happy they are delirious. I have never been to a male strip club where the customers got so excited. It just goes to show you what birds are really like. They like it more than you do, most of them.

'Can I take something off?' The bird who says this is quite attractive and I reckon that she must be talking about my clobber.

'Be my guest,' I say, extending the troublesome Kicker.

Thirty seconds later, the troublesome Kicker is still firmly attached to my foot and the bird is down to her bra and panties. 'Don't!' I say. 'You mustn't! No!'

But it is no good. She rips off her bra and shakes her knockers like she is trying to flick drops of water off them. I wish she would not do that. The effect on percy is most distressing. Always on the impulsive side and inclined to show off in front of large groups of people he is coming up a lot faster than Reginald Dixon's organ. The effect of the bird's performance on the rest of the audience is also distressing. Never, what you might call, restrained, they are now baying like a pack of hounds at feeding time.

'Give him one, Doreen!'

'Get your trousers off!'

'Get on with it!'

I never thought that bingo sessions were what women really wanted but this is ridiculous. A lot of pent up emotion is threatening to burst in a tidal wave of sexual violence. I know because I have seen the posters outside the cinemas.

'Come on my lap!' I think the woman means 'sit on my lap' but you never know with this lot. I am being bundled about like a packet of chips at a miser's convention. Another pair of hands seize hold of me while the frustrated strip-teaser prances about stark bollock naked on the platform.

'You're a tease, aren't you?' says my new friend. 'Show us what you've got. Go on, don't mess about.' She starts fiddling with the zip on my trousers.

'I'll help you, May.' The speaker is not the only one to step forward and before you can say Roger Carpenter both my shoes have been wrenched off – I expect to see my foot in one of them. Strong fingers – no doubt all that work on the looms helps – yanks my trousers over my knees.

'Thank you, ladies,' I say making one of the most unheartfelt statements of my life.

I am now down to my fleas and ants and it is only with the greatest difficulty that I tear myself free and scramble to my feet. If I have got to sit on every lap in the room I might as well forget any thoughts of ever becoming a father. Better to retreat to the stage. The encumbant bird, is probably only interested in flashing herself about a bit. I expect she does it in front of the wardrobe mirror at home when her old man is on nights. Percy is not exactly playing dormice down the front of my Y-fronts and I have to endure some very embarrassing comments as I hop up on the stage. I don't know how the professionals keep their emotions under control. It must come with practice – or, more likely, not come with practice.

'Give him one, Doreen!'

I do wish that woman would belt up. Doreen has got enough on her mind without getting any more ideas. While

I try and strike a muscleman pose she willows towards me and slides her arms round my waist. I drop my arms sharpish as her fingers fluster my cluster.

'Come on,' she says. 'Let's do it.'

'You must be mad!' I hiss. 'Get off the stage.'

'Go on.' Her hands are inside my Y-fronts. It is terrible. I have to pull her to me to stop everybody seeing.

'Don't be shy.' She flips down my pants at the back and a big cheer goes up. I move my hands to deal with the problem and she tugs down the front. Now it is a question of 'Missile ready for firing, sir'. I try to keep percy hidden but she rolls her body from side to side so he plays peek-a-boo with the audience. Talk about embarrassing. I don't know where to put myself – or do I? Maybe, to put it in would be the easiest way out. At least I would not have to look at all those birds taking the piss out of me. Even as I gaze into the gloom, another one of them starts pulling off her blouse. Doreen begins to run her open mouth along my shoulder and that helps make up my mind. I will concentrate on her and shut out the rest of them. Maybe that will satisfy them. Who knows? It might even satisfy me. I take her underneath the shoulders and lay her down on the stage keeping as close to her as I can. In the background, I can hear the noise of breaking furniture. I hope I am doing the right thing. At least, one person seems to think I am. Doreen's mouth jumps open as I dunk my doughnut filler and she closes her eyes.

'That's heaven!' she purrs. Closing my ears to the riot about I proceed with the work that nature intended me for: in-out, in-out, in-out, in—

To my left are the bongos and, presumably, near them is the panic button. Never one to take chances, I begin to hump Doreen towards what I imagine to be safety. The jostle round the platform makes a Rolling Stones concert seem like the vicar's knobbly knees contest at the village fete.

'Move over, Doreen.'

'You've had your fun.'

'I was here first!'

'Watch it!'

'I warned you!'

All of a sudden, I find myself trying to do my bit – Doreen, you remember her? – between a forest of female legs, quite a few of them naked and attached to other parts of the body in a very similar condition.

'Help!' I scream as hands that have never, I swear, experienced the soft kiss of Fairy Liquid plunder my defenceless body. 'HELP!!!!'

It is not often that I resort to a four exclamation mark scream but in this situation I have to. What lies between my legs may not be fantasy material but I like it just the way it is – and where it is! 'HELP!!!!'

For once in my life, a cry from the heart – or, in this case, somewhat lower down – is answered.

'Get off him!' That is a man's voice.

'He's not a member of EQUITY. I've never seen him before!' That is also a man's voice – at least, I think it is. I turn my head to see Brownlow and a geezer in what looks like a butch version of a Batman costume with 'Mr Show-All' embroidered across his concave chest.

'Thank God you've come!' I gasp.

A long drawn-out moan from beneath me suggests that someone else has come as well.

CHAPTER TEN

In which snow falls and Timmy comes across an old friend.

After that it all gets a bit confusing. I remember Brownlow being raped and Mr Show-All demanding to see my union card but after the woman called Winnie starts to do the incredible trick with the bongo drum – I do hope they get it back – my memory becomes a bit suspect. Why all the blokes started smashing the place up I don't know. I think at the time I thought it had something to do with them being worried about their old ladies having it away with Mr Show-All. That would account for them throwing him in the canal – not bad when you think that the canal was fifty yards away and that they didn't leave the room to do it – didn't even open the window in fact. It's a good job I was lying under one of the tables at the time.

Of course the really terrible thing is what happens to my load of glasses. Yes, somehow they find their way to them and every single one of them is smashed. Most of the glasses are smashed as well. It wouldn't be so bad if I'd come to the right club. Awful, isn't it? All these towns look alike and they all run into each other – they look as if they've run into something, anyway – I'm sorry, I shouldn't have said that. Balham High Street doesn't look so hot on a rainy Monday – doesn't look so hot on Christmas Day with the sun shining, either.

Of course, Brownlow doesn't want to know about my problems. I try and have a word with him as they put him in the ambulance but he tells me to – no, I won't tell you what he tells me to do because if you are sensitive it will upset you as much as it did me.

I could accept it all more easily if it had been my fault. Honestly, there is no justice. I bent over backwards to bring a little pleasure to those women – forwards on a couple of occasions, I know for a fact that Sid will kill me when I get back to London. It was necessary to take out a special insurance to cover the glasses and he didn't have time to do it – because of the rush nature of the job and his natural meaness. We must be in hock for hundreds of quid, now. Enough to bankrupt the business.

I sweep the last bits of broken glass out of the back of the lorry and wonder what to do. I am supposed to pick up a load of sheepskins from Carlisle and take them over to Hull but in my present frame of mind I feel like packing the whole thing in. Still, you can't let people down, can you? And at least it will put off my interview with Sid.

In the end, I have a cup of tea and push on up the M6. There is no point in going to the factory so I spend the night in the cab. Bleeding cold and uncomfortable it is. The trouble is that I don't feel entitled to spend money on a night's sleep after what happened to the load. It is amazing how pangs of conscience can catch up with you sometimes.

The next morning, the sky is darker than a Hashamite's hampton and there is a cobbler-creaking wind trying to rush up my trouser leg. It is also cold. Very cold. By the time I have picked up the sheepskins and headed into the Pennine Hills, brass monkeys are conspicuous by their absence. The tops of the peaks are white and there is a coating of the stuff further down the slopes. Everybody on the road seems to be hurrying as if they want to get off it fast and you don't have to be a BBC Weatherman to reckon that there is a lot more snow in the air. A sports car goes past me with its horn screaming. 'Get out of it!' and I give him a toot wishing that the button in the middle of the steering wheel worked a missile launcher. I can't help thinking about Sid and what I am going to say to him. Maybe I ought to ring him? I suppose the blokes who were expecting the glasses must be getting a bit worried by now. Maybe I ought to ring them?

As if I did not have enough on my mind, it suddenly starts to snow. Not a few pretty flakes but a wall of the stuff that shuts out any view of the hills and cuts visibility to a few yards. The windscreen wipers can hardly cope with it. When the wind gets behind it, it travels parallel to the ground. And what a wind! The superstructure of the lorry shudders like it is about to buckle and I can hardly hold Enid on the road. If I had known it was going to be like this I would have joined the French Foreign Legion. I press my face up against the windscreen and decide that I will stop at the next village I come to – if I can get that far. The snow is banking up against the side of the road and rippling across it as if it is fast-flowing water stirred into eddies and currents by the wind. I come round a corner and nearly bash into the back of the sports car that overtook me a few miles back. It must have run out of road. Its front bumper is wedged up against a stone wall and a geezer in a peak cap is standing beside it, hunched up against the bizzard.

I stop and wind the window down. 'Can you move it?'

The bloke shakes his head. 'The fender's bent in against the tyre.'

'Do you want a lift?' A figure starts to climb out of the passenger seat.

'No thanks. I'd better stay here. Stop at the next garage and tell them I'm here, will you?'

'Right.'

We are both having to shout to make ourselves heard. The snow is stinging my face like grit.

'I'll come with you.'

At first, I don't recognise the bird climbing in beside me. She has a scarf tied round her nut.

'Are you sure you want to stay?' I yell at the bloke.

Since I had been talking to him a foot of snow has built up against the side of his car.

'I don't want to leave it.'

'Please yourself. Good luck.' I pull the door shut and the noise level drops by half. The bird is shaking snow out of her hair and I start coaxing Enid forward. 'I'll drop you at the garage,' I say. 'You can wait there.'

'I'm not with him,' says the bird. 'He was only giving me a lift.'

I turn and look at her and she stops running her hand through her barnet. 'Well, well. Small world, isn't it?'

'How long can we go on meeting like this?' I say. 'Did you have a nice time with the Fuzz?'

Shirl brushes some snow off her scarf. 'All right.'

There doesn't seem to be a lot to say to that so I concentrate on the road – or what I can see of it. The whole scene is a detergent manufacturer's dream: whiter than whiter than white.

'This is bloody stupid,' I say. 'We can't go on like this.'

'Are you talking about us or the road?' says Shirl.

I run up what turns out to be the verge and we both bang our bonces on the roof of the cab. 'The road,' I say. 'We'll have to stop. I can't see a blooming thing.'

I pull up as close to a stone wall as I can and turn off the engine. 'It's going to be as cold in this as it was in the other one,' says Shirl, pulling her coat around her,

'We'll get in the back,' I say. 'I'm carrying a load of sheepskins.'

'What are you smiling about?' says Shirl.

'I was just thinking,' I say.

'Oh.' Shirl raises one of her eyebrows a sixteenth of an inch.

'We might be here for days,' I say. 'Look how it's building up out there.'

'Have you got anything to eat?' I shake my head. Shirl looks in her bag. 'I've got a bar of chocolate and an apple.'

'We'll have to spin it out,' I say. 'At least we'll be warm.'

'Yeah, that's something, isn't it?' We look into each other's eyes for a few long moments and Shirl leans forward and combs my beard with her finger nails. 'You're looking forward to it, aren't you?'

'In a way,' I say.

Shirl kisses me lightly on the lips. 'So am I. Come on, let's get in the back before the snow gets too deep.'

CONFESSIONS FROM THE POP SCENE

Timothy Lea

Teenyboppers, hungry groupies, payola, crooked DJs, foreign tours, golden discs, TV spectaculars, screaming fans and packed out concert halls...

For Timmy Lea, always on the lookout for a new career with plenty of openings, Noggo Enterprises spelled success, money and a chance to get his name into the bright lights – providing he could survive the partnership with brother-in-law Sid and his nephew Jason Noggett, the 7-year-old's answer to Mick Jagger, not to speak of Dyke Henna, the transvestite rock star (born Fred Nudger).

Even when business was slow, the manager of Noggo Enterprises found plenty of scope for his talents; in beds, bars and the back seats of sportscars there was always somebody who wanted a little piece of his action.

Would simple, unaffected Timmy survive in the hard world of Pop?